OSLG

D1430194

LATE FOR GETTYSBURG

Though the Civil War is over, former Confederate soldier Eugene Wyeth refuses to forgive and forget. Living under an assumed name with a price on his head, he wanders the country, anticipating a bounty hunter around every corner. But when his old comrade-in-arms Rattlesnake Jack is shot, Wyeth must risk exposure and ride into town to seek help. With the powerful Kirby Taylor and his gang of gunslingers determined to stand in Wyeth's way, there is trouble looming.

*Books by Vance Tillman
in the Linford Western Library:*

RIDERS ON THE WIND
DUST AND BULLETS

VANCE TILLMAN

LATE FOR GETTYSBURG

Complete and Unabridged

LINFORD
Leicester

First published in Great Britain in 2013 by
Robert Hale Limited
London

First Linford Edition
published 2015
by arrangement with
Robert Hale Limited
London

A catalogue record for this book is available
from the British Library.

ISBN 978–1–4448–2611–1

Published by
F. A. Thorpe (Publishing)
Anstey, Leicestershire

Set by Words & Graphics Ltd.
Anstey, Leicestershire
Printed and bound in Great Britain by
T. J. International Ltd., Padstow, Cornwall

This book is printed on acid-free paper

1

Eugene Wyeth wasn't his real name, but he had become so used to it that it seemed he had never been called anything else. Originally, he had chosen it to protect his family. It probably wouldn't help much. He didn't trust the Federals any more now that the war had ended than he had when it was being fought. Other people might forgive, even his own family, but not he. As far as he was concerned, the war continued.

He rode at a steady pace in order to conserve his horse. The steeldust mare had been with him for a long time, through most of the war. They had a rapport. They understood each other. What was more, Wyeth reckoned that she hated Yankees as much as he did. Ahead of them the trail wound like a snake. The sun shone out of a high blue heaven but a cool breeze rippled the grass. He began to recognize some of the familiar landmarks. Scattered cottonwood and willow indicated the line of Winding Creek. In another score of miles he would be at the town of Winding where his brother ran the general store and his sister taught school. He was looking forward to sampling his ma's cooking. Only his pa was missing; lost at Corinth early in the war. Yet the others seemed to have come to terms with the new regime. He had tried but he couldn't do it.

It was mid-afternoon when he clattered across the loose planks of the bridge at the end of town and entered the main street. The place seemed to have grown since he was last there. There were more shops and stores than he remembered and the buildings seemed somehow to have grown taller. As he approached the general store he slowed down. He had intended calling on his brother first but he changed his mind and rode on. The main street of false-fronted structures led to a small central square shaded by trees. A couple of old-timers sat on a bench; a dog sprawled lazily at their feet. One of the oldsters raised a hand in greeting. Wyeth continued till he came to a side street of substantial frame houses with gardens. He dismounted outside one of them and, tying the horse to the fence, opened the wicket gate and walked slowly up the path. Before he had reached the door it was flung open and a big-bosomed lady with white hair drawn back in a bun rushed out on to the veranda.

'Sam!' she exclaimed.

He bounded up the steps and took her in his arms. After a few moments he held his mother away from him.

'Remember not to call me Sam,' he said. 'Sam Holland doesn't exist any more. Remember, he got killed in the war.'

'Oh, fiddlesticks. What can it matter? There's nobody around, just you and me.'

'It don't signify. Better get into the habit of calling me Eugene. It's safer that way.'

'And am I supposed to act as though you're not my son? I'll never be able to do that.'

Wyeth didn't reply and his mother, sensing that she might have started on the wrong tack, turned the conversation to something more matter of fact. 'You're a funny one. Where have you just come from this time?'

'Up around a place called Cold Creek. I have to be back there, but I got some time.' He smiled down at his mother's upturned face and took her hand. 'Come on, let's go inside.'

The room they entered was pleasant. There were flowers in vases and on the walls hung a sampler, which his sister had made as a girl.

'Make yourself comfortable,' his mother said. 'I reckon you could probably do with something to eat?'

'You read my thoughts,' Wyeth replied. 'At nights I dream of your meat pie.'

'Then you're in luck. I got a Cousin Jack pasty just ready to take out of the oven. I was intendin' it for later but there's plenty to go round.'

'What time are you expectin' Shelby and Kate back?'

'Kate shouldn't be too long. Shelby tends to keep long hours at the store.'

Wyeth thought for a moment. 'Why don't we all go along and see him later if he's not back in good time?'

His mother smiled. 'Why, that would be real nice,' she said. She was obviously pleased at the suggestion but Wyeth felt there was something else behind it. He thought he knew what it was.

'Like I said, I could stay awhiles,' he shouted as she retreated into the kitchen.

'That would be real nice too,' she called back. 'While you're eatin', I'll go and make up a bed.'

★   ★   ★

Shelby Holland's general store was the largest in town. It stocked all the main items anyone was likely to need and in addition, Shelby had branched out. With due regard to the businesses of his neighbours, as well as groceries he also stocked items of hardware and drugs such as laudanum for general aches and pains, oil of peppermint for stomach complaints, turpentine, beeswax and coal oil. At the moment in which his brother was tucking into his meal, he was summoned from the storeroom by the tinkling of the bell above the outer door. A man entered but didn't immediately move to the counter. Instead, after standing inside the doorway for a few moments, glancing round as he did so, he began to circle the shop, looking at the items on display.

Shelby had time to observe him more closely. He was not one of his usual customers and Shelby did not recognize him. He was slightly taller than average and wore the usual range gear. There was nothing distinctive about him except that he walked with a slight limp. He carried two guns. That was unusual. Most folks, if they carried a gun at all, usually packed only one. And since Marshal Snider had taken office, guns had been banned in public places.

'Can I be of help?' Holland asked.

The man turned and approached him. His flat eyes slid over and behind the counter before focusing on Holland.

'Tobacco,' he said. As Holland reached along the shelf, he could feel the stranger's eyes on his back. 'Do you know of a decent hotel?' the man said.

'Sure. In fact there are a couple, the Alhambra and the Spur. But if you're lookin' for somethin' more cosy, I would recommend the Willow House.'

'How do I get there?' the man said.

'The Willow House? Just carry on right along Main Street till you come to the town square. It's over in the right hand corner.'

The man nodded, paid for his tobacco and walked back through the door into the street. Holland paused for a moment before moving quickly to the window. The stranger was walking slowly in the direction he had indicated. For some reason, he suddenly felt uneasy. He had recommended the Willow House because it was run by Magenta Kirkwood. She had been a friend of his mother's for a long time. His intentions had been good, but now he wished he hadn't suggested it.

⋆　⋆　⋆

When he had finished his meal, Wyeth sat on the veranda with his mother.

'You don't mind if I smoke?' he asked.

'Of course not. Your father always used to smoke a pipe. A meerschaum it was. I don't know where he got it from.'

'Yes, I remember,' Wyeth replied. He took out his pack of Bull Durham and rolled a cigarette. 'That was some meal,' he said, 'it's really good to be home.'

His mother did not answer for a while. Wyeth took a long drag, waiting for what was coming next.

'You could come back for good,' she said at last. 'You don't have to be a wanderer.'

'You know that's not true,' he replied.

'Why can't it be true? It's true for other people.'

'You know why. I'm a wanted man with a price on my head.'

'You could give yourself up. Surely they'd be lenient with you if you handed yourself in. You tell me you haven't ever killed anybody. There are people who would speak up for you.'

'I can't. It's too late. Besides, I wouldn't want to.'

She gave him a look of exasperation. 'Why couldn't you be like everyone else? There's Jim Reynolds and Bob Adams. They were with you during the war. Look at them now. They're well set up on their own farms. What makes you so different?'

'I don't want to talk about it, Ma.'

'The war is over. What's past is past.'

'Is that how you feel about Pa?' he snapped. He saw the look of distress on his mother's face. 'I'm sorry,' he said. 'I didn't mean to upset you.' He got to his feet and, bending down, took his mother into his arms. 'Come on, let's not go over all this again. Let's just enjoy bein' together.'

He held her tightly for a few moments until he heard footsteps and his sister appeared on the road in front of the house. She stopped for a moment, uncertain of who it was on the veranda, and then, realizing it was her brother, she ran up the path.

'Hello, Sis,' he said.

'Sam! I didn't expect to see you.'

'I figured it was about time I paid a visit,' he replied.

'How long are you here for?'

'That depends. I'm not in any great hurry.'

His mother had got to her feet and dried her eyes. Wyeth turned to her. 'Say,' he said, 'why don't we do like we said earlier and all go see Shelby?'

'I expect Kate must be tired,' his mother replied. 'It's not easy coping with those kids all day.'

Kate laughed. 'I'm fine,' she said. 'Goodness, anyone would think I'd spent the day down a mine or something. I'd say that was an excellent idea. Come on. Let's go right now.'

★   ★   ★

Kirby Taylor was a big name in the town of Cold Creek. He stood by the window of his office looking down on the street. The town was busy. Cold Creek was on the up and business was booming. What was good for Cold Creek was good for Kirby Taylor, since he owned a good part of it, his most recent acquisition being the stagecoach line. He couldn't help a little smirk of satisfaction lifting the corners of his mouth. There was a knock on the door and it opened to admit his secretary.

'Someone to see you,' she said. 'He says he's expected.'

The grin on Taylor's face widened. 'Thank you, Miss Hoskins. You can show him in.'

After a few moments a small man with a bald head entered. Taylor showed him to a chair and then took his place at a roll-top desk opposite. Taylor looked the man up and down but waited for him to speak. The man shifted uncomfortably in his chair.

'Mr Taylor,' he said, 'I did like you told me.'

Taylor sat back and stretched out his arms. 'Your name's Hobbs, isn't it,' he said inconsequentially. The man nodded. Taylor looked him up and down. 'Well, go on. What have you got to report?'

'Mr Taylor,' the man said, 'I did just like you told me to. I've been spreading the word about the payroll.'

'You're sure you made it quite clear?'

'Yes. I reckon most folks in town must know about it now.'

'You mentioned dates and times for the stagecoach?'

'Yes.' He shifted uncomfortably. 'I don't mean to question your instructions, but isn't it rather unwise to give out that sort of information?'

Taylor suddenly jerked forward. The smile was gone from his face. 'You don't question anything I tell you to do,' he snapped. 'You understand? You carry out your orders.'

'I'm sorry, Mr Taylor. I didn't mean — '

'Just hear what I say and don't ask questions. If you know what's good for you, that is.'

The man shrank away. Taylor reached out a hand and took a cigar from a box on the table but didn't offer one to the other man.

'You've done OK,' he said after cutting and lighting it. 'I believe I can recommend you, should a position ever arise for a senior clerk.'

The man remained sitting for a moment as though he expected something more. As Taylor sat back and blew a ring of smoke into the air he seemed to get the message that the interview was over. He got to his feet.

'Thank you, Mr Taylor,' he said. 'If there's anything else — '

'Rest assured, you're the first person I would contact.'

Cringingly, Hobbs moved towards the door. 'Goodbye, Mr Taylor.'

Taylor didn't respond as the man opened the door silently and slithered through. When he heard the outer door close Taylor rose and went back to the window. After a few moments the man appeared and he watched him as he moved along the boardwalk, disappearing eventually into the stage depot. Taylor turned and, putting on his frock coat, left the room.

'Why don't you take the rest of the day off?' he said to his secretary. After his brief meeting, he was feeling expansive. The word about the payroll had been spread. With any luck it would reach its proper target. He knew there were Confederate outlaws in the area, among them former members of Jeb Stuart's cavalry. The fact that they carried on fighting a dead campaign did not excuse them for previous treachery. The Black Skull would deal with them.

'Are you sure you won't be needing me for anything?' Miss Hoskins was saying.

'I always need you,' Taylor beamed, 'but the rest of this afternoon is yours to enjoy.'

She got to her feet. Not for the first time Taylor admired the thrust of her breasts beneath the tight blouse. She stood for a moment as if undecided. Taylor smiled, took her arm and together they walked down the stairs and into the street.

★   ★   ★

The man who had been in Shelby Holland's store locked the door of his room in the Willow House boarding establishment and then threw himself down on the bed. For a long time he lay unmoving, looking up at the ceiling. Then he sat up and, reaching into an inside pocket, produced a flask of whiskey together with a crumpled sheet of paper. He put the flask to his lips and took a good long pull. He spluttered slightly before taking another. He laid the flask aside and unfolded the sheet of paper. There was a picture on it and some writing. He glanced briefly at the picture and then read what was written beneath it.

Eugene Wyeth. Age twenty-six. Medium height and build. Distinctive marks: none. Refused amnesty and wanted by US Military. Previously served as guerrilla with James Ewell Brown 'Jeb' Stuart, Cavalry Corps, Army of Northern Virginia. Wanted subsequently for robbery and murder. Two thousand dollar reward. Dead or alive.

When he had finished reading it through several times, he folded it up and put it back in his pocket. He strolled to the window and looked down on the square. Darkness was falling and lights were appearing. He couldn't be sure, but he was pretty certain that the man he had trailed to Winding was the man on the Wanted poster. It had been a stroke of luck that he had run into him at a trading store on the Wilderness River. He wasn't certain that Wyeth was in town, but there was no other town within a considerable distance. It wasn't a problem. If he was right, all he had to do was hang about long enough for Wyeth to show. He wasn't concerned about the reward, although it might be worth taking up. It would certainly be the easiest two thousand dollars he was ever likely to earn. But he had other business. Either way, he didn't intend on messing about. The poster gave him a choice but there was no choice as far as he was concerned. Wyeth was going to die.

* * *

After the initial discussion with his mother, the subject of Wyeth's situation was avoided by all members of the family. The following morning, after Shelby had left early to go to the store, Wyeth accompanied his sister to the school. It was a small white building on the opposite side of town with space for only two classrooms. Kate took a senior class in one of them while an elderly woman took the junior class in the other.

'The arrangement isn't a fixed one,' she said. 'There is quite a lot of movement. For example, if a student does well in the junior class in a certain subject, he might be moved up to the senior class in that same subject.'

'And vice versa?' Wyeth commented.

'Yes. It can make for complications, but it seems to work.'

After he left his sister, Wyeth returned to the livery stables and saddled up. He took a different trail out of town to that on which he had ridden in. It was good to be with his folks, but already he was feeling something of a strain and he wanted to clear his mind. He had spent too long on the run, moving from place to place and sleeping under the stars, not to feel cramped when he had a roof over his head or stayed very long in one place. He was aware he was taking something of a risk in returning to Winding. That didn't worry him. He would be concerned if his family were to be put at any risk, but that didn't seem likely. It was true what his mother had said. Sure, he had robbed banks and stagecoaches, but nobody except himself had ever got hurt. That Wanted poster they had distributed was telling a damn lie when it put him down for murder. And for all his escapades, he had hardly a dime himself to show for it. On the other hand, there were plenty of hungry families, destitute farmers and wounded greybacks that had a lot to thank him for. Yes, and others, too.

His thoughts ran on and it was not till he began to see cattle on the range that he realized he was on Barbed R property. He had not intended riding that way, but now he was on the Rawley spread he found himself facing a decision. Should he ride on and pay a call? He sat for a while considering the problem. When he had left Jolie the last time, he had determined not to see her again; his way of life ruled out a lasting relationship. What could he offer her? A life on the run was no life at all for a young woman. It was only fair to her that he leave her alone to find someone else. He knew the answer to his question. It would do no one any good to call. Better to accept the situation. Yet his every instinct was to see her one more time.

He had just about resolved the issue and was ready to start back for town when the decision was taken out of his hands. It was an indication of how lost in thought he had been that he failed to hear the sound of wheels till the buggy was almost upon him. It had come up over the crest of a low hill, which had served to drown the sound. He looked up sharply and his heart skipped a beat. Jolie herself was in the driving seat. She seemed to see him late as she brought the buggy to a sudden halt. She apparently did not immediately recognize the rider in her path, but when she did she gave a cry and jumped down from the buggy. Wyeth slid from the saddle. When they were close she stopped and they both suddenly felt awkward. It was the girl who broke the silence.

'Sam! What are you doing here? It's seems so long since I saw you. Were you on your way to visit?'

'Yes,' Wyeth lied.

She gave him an uncertain look. 'Have you seen your folks? Are you staying with them?'

'I just got here yesterday.'

She looked him up and down. 'You look thin,' she said. 'It's good that you're here. You need feeding up.'

Wyeth grinned. 'Ma's already started.'

He didn't know what to say. Events seemed to have taken a turn of their own. He had not intended riding to the Barbed R. It seemed he had done so unconsciously. Having arrived there, he had not planned on meeting Jolie. Yet here she was. It was as if some kind of providence had been guiding him and he was all unprepared. Apart from that, the way Jolie looked would have floored him. She was more beautiful even than he remembered her. Maybe it was because she looked so natural. She wore a hat but her long auburn hair had come loose and blew in the breeze. She was dressed in a casual riding outfit, which, for all its plainness, only served to emphasize the outlines of her fine figure.

'Well,' she said, 'I guess we're not doing a lot of good standing here. Let's get on to the ranch house. My father will be pleased to see you. He's out fixing some fences. That's where I've been, taking his food. But he shouldn't be too late back.'

Wyeth nodded and they stood for a moment, hesitating. She turned towards the buggy and he moved quickly to help her into the driver's seat. As he took her hand she turned to face him and suddenly he forgot all his previous resolves and took her in his arms. She did not resist as her lips hungrily sought his. For a long time they remained pressed together till at last she gently pushed him away. Her face was flushed and her eyes glistening.

'I've been dreaming of you doing that ever since you went away,' she panted.

'I'm sorry,' he began, but she put a finger to his lips to stop him. 'Don't say anything. Just hold me tight once more.'

He didn't need a second invitation. When they finally drew apart she whispered: 'Ride alongside me.'

Wyeth was torn. He wanted to do as she said and ride back with her, but instinctively he held back. In the brief time she took stepping into the buggy and taking up the reins, he wrestled with his emotions. Things had taken such an unexpected turn. He didn't know how to deal with his feelings. Through it all one thought worried him. Jolie had said that her father would be glad to see him, but he wasn't so sure. Joe Rawley had been as keen a supporter of the Confederacy as any man and had seen his own share of action during the war. But Wyeth knew that didn't guarantee him a favourable reception. He was pretty sure that Rawley did not know about the things he had been up to or that he was now a wanted man, but it wouldn't be natural if he didn't have his suspicions. Quite apart from that, Rawley, as a father, could hardly approve of Wyeth's relationship with his daughter. Quickly, Wyeth came to a decision.

'I don't think it would be a good idea for me to come back with you to the ranch house.'

The difficulty it cost him in saying the words was matched by the look of pain that blanched her features. It was a fleeting moment and she quickly recovered herself.

'When will I see you?' she said.

'I don't know. You must understand — '

'I don't want to understand. I want — ' She stopped and then looked up at him imploringly. 'Come and see me again if you can. Before you go.' He turned away and swung himself into the saddle. The steeldust sidled a few paces.

'Sam Holland, you just make sure you take care of yourself,' she said. The next instant she flicked the reins and the buggy went trundling away, its wheels raising a thin cloud of dust. He sat his horse for a time, not moving until the buggy was out of sight. Then he touched his spurs to the steeldust's flanks and set off slowly down the trail in the opposite direction.

He hadn't been riding for long when he saw a small dust cloud coming up on his right. He took a quick look around. There was a draw a little way ahead marked by a few willow trees and he rode into their shelter. After a time a lone rider appeared. He seemed to be heading towards the Barbed R and Wyeth relaxed, confident that he was in all likelihood a Barbed R ranch-hand. He remained in concealment till the rider was out of sight. Seeing the man come by served to remind him that just lately he had been getting a little careless. Maybe it had been a bad idea to come on this visit. Maybe it was self-indulgence. He needed to sharpen up, get back in action. That was the way to salvation. That way, he might numb the pain that gnawed at him since he had torn himself apart from Jolie. He would stay for just another day or two. He owed his mother at least that. He felt a stab of remorse. She had obviously been hoping he might stay longer. It would be difficult to leave, but it had to be done.

He already had a vague plan in mind, something he had been considering for a while: the Cold Creek stage. His old comrade in arms, Rattlesnake Jack, had heard a rumour that the stage regularly carried bullion for the bank at Cold Creek, money which would be used to pay Federal soldiers. In fact, Rattlesnake had the information from an employee of the stage company itself. He would get back to the old-timer and work out the details with him. Hell, it would be good to see him again. The oldster was as quick and deadly as a rattlesnake with a gun or a knife, but that wasn't how he had earned his soubriquet. He had done that the day he seized an axe and chopped off the two fingers of his left hand that had been bitten by a rattlesnake. Wyeth was already feeling better just thinking about him. With a last glance around, he moved out from the shelter of the trees and started back for Winding.

2

Shelby Holland glanced out of the window of his shop the morning following his brother's arrival. It was early and the streets were quiet so he was surprised to see the stranger who had been in his shop previously already up and about and making his way down the dusty street. He watched as the stranger turned into the livery stables. Just then the bell tinkled over the door and he had to move away to serve a customer.

As he entered the stables, the stranger took a moment for his eyes to adjust to the comparative gloom. The ostler appeared from somewhere at the back.

'Howdy,' he said. 'Come to check your horse?' There was no reply. 'Sure looks like it's goin' to be a hot day.'

The stranger ignored him and wandered down the line of stalls. His own

28

horse looked up as he passed but he didn't stop. Instead his eyes fell on a big black steeldust a couple of stalls further on.

'That's a nice horse,' he said.

'Sure is.'

'Does it belong to somebody in town?'

'That horse? Nope. Belongs to a fella came by just recently. Say, you're a stranger in town yourself, ain't you? Stayin' at the Alhambra?'

'Nope.'

'Well, it's a nice town. You visitin'?'

The stranger did not reply. He examined the horse more closely.

'Sure is goin' to be a hot day,' the ostler drawled. He came closer. 'Name's Wellman,' he said, 'Amos Wellman.' He held out a hand. The stranger did not take it. The ostler hesitated a moment before dropping his outstretched arm. It was clear that the conversation was at an end. Turning on his heel and brushing past the ostler, the stranger walked slowly out of the stables and into the sunlight. The ostler was right. It was already hot out in the street. He needed a drink. He began to walk in the direction of the Horseshoe saloon but when he got there it was closed. Instead he made his way further down the street to Sloane's eating house, went inside and ordered coffee.

He had only taken a couple of sips when the door opened and the marshal appeared. He came across to the stranger's table and, pulling out a chair, sat opposite him. For a moment neither spoke. The waitress approached the table but the marshal shook his head. When she had gone away, he turned to the stranger.

'Let me introduce myself,' he said. 'I'm Marshal Snider.' The man did not reply. 'I take it you got a name?'

The man gave the marshal a hard stare. 'Gray,' he replied.

'You got business in Winding?'

'What's that to you?' Gray responded. 'I ain't breakin' no laws.'

The marshal grinned. 'Now that's just where you're wrong,' he said.

'What do you mean?'

'We got an ordinance in Winding that says you have to check in your guns when you hit town. For as long as you're in town. Introduced it myself. I couldn't help but notice you're carryin' side arms.'

'I didn't see any notice.'

The marshal ignored him. 'I guess you won't have any objection to handing them over. You can collect 'em when you leave town.'

Gray looked out of the window. The street was busier. A number of people were passing one another along the sidewalks; horses were tethered at some of the hitch-racks and further down the street a wagon was drawn up outside the County Courthouse. The marshal observed him closely. He knew the type. What was he doing in Winding? He wasn't concerned because the man wasn't going to be staying long. Gray seemed to be wrestling with some

31

thought. Finally, reluctantly, he turned back and, drawing his guns, handed them to the marshal.

'I'll take care of 'em,' Snider said. 'Like I say, you can collect 'em when you leave town.' He got to his feet and strode to the door. 'Oh, and by the way,' he said, 'That'll be by noon tomorrow.'

* * *

Wyeth did not mention anything of his meeting with Jolie Rawley to his mother and they both seemed to go out of their way to avoid any controversial subjects. They spent the day together until his sister and brother returned later. Shelby had left the store early for once to spend more time with his brother. As they sat together that evening Wyeth was content to listen to Shelby and Kate as they talked about their day.

'It's kinda funny,' Shelby said. 'I had a fella in the store yesterday. I'd never seen him before. I figured he must be just passin' through. Then I took a look out the window this mornin' and there he was, walkin' down the street. Since then I've seen him a few times. He was sittin' on a rail outside the Horseshoe saloon when I came past on my way here, talkin' with another man.'

'Sounds like he's just wasting time. Maybe he's waiting to meet someone,' Kate remarked.

'He don't look the type.'

'What type does he look like?' their mother asked.

'A bit mean. He was carryin' side arms when he came by the store.'

'In that case, the marshal will be havin' a word with him,' their mother said.

'I guess he must be stayin' a while because he's puttin' up at the Willow House. I suggested it myself. I ain't sure now whether that was a good idea.'

Wyeth had been listening without saying anything. Now he turned to his brother. 'Why do you say that?' he asked.

'Well, like I said, he looked mean.'

'Mean?'

'I don't know. Like a weasel. I didn't like the look of him. Come to think of it, I didn't like the look of the fella I saw him talkin' with, either.'

'Well, we don't have to worry about him,' their mother said. 'If there's anything not right about him, Marshal Snider will deal with it.'

'He's a good man, this Snider?' Wyeth asked.

'Very good. The town has been real peaceable since he took over.'

The conversation took a different turn and the subject of the stranger was forgotten. Only Wyeth was left with something to ponder.

★   ★   ★

Night fell. In his room at the Willow House, Gray was pacing up and down. His encounter with the marshal had left him fuming and nothing had happened during the course of the day to make him feel any happier. All day he had hung about town, hoping to catch a glimpse of Wyeth, but without success. Now his hand was being forced. It seemed the marshal had taken an objection to him and wanted him out of town. If he was true to his word, that meant he had to be gone by noon tomorrow. Maybe he was bluffing? No, there was something about the marshal that told him he wasn't the type to bluff. If he told someone to be gone by a certain time, he meant it. Which meant he had to act quickly. So what was he to do?

After a time he suddenly stopped and sat on the bed. He had come to a decision. He knew that Wyeth was definitely in town because he recognized his horse. It was a good horse. What would happen if it disappeared? Wyeth wouldn't be likely to just let it go. He would come looking for it. All he had to do was take the horse, leave a clear trail and then set himself up to drygulch Wyeth when he showed up.

The only problem would be stealing the horse, but that shouldn't be too difficult. He could carry it out tonight and have plenty of time to set himself up for the kill. It was a pity the marshal had his guns, but he still had his rifle. He could even double back to town early in the morning after he had set himself up and collect the guns from the marshal. Yes, he liked the irony of it. The more he thought the plan over, the better he liked it. It made a lot of sense, too, to carry out the killing away from town. He had envisaged the option of taking a pot-shot from an alley, but when he thought about it, there were too many chances, too many imponderables to a scheme like that. Things could go wrong; there could be awkward consequences. No, this was much better. This way he had complete control. He could meet Wyeth at a place of his own choosing and he knew just the sort of setup he wanted.

★   ★   ★

Quite early the next morning, Wyeth paid a visit to the Willow House. He was met by Magenta Kirkwood.

'Sam,' she said. 'How long have you been back?'

'A coupla days. I'm just visitin'.'

She stood back to regard him. 'You look as handsome as ever. Your ma must sure be glad to see you. Come on in. What brings you to the Willow House, anyway?'

When Wyeth mentioned the stranger who had been in his brother's shop, Magenta nodded.

'I agree with Shelby,' she said. 'I can't say as I took to him. Not that I've any cause for complaint. He paid up in advance and if he's decided to go already, that's his prerogative.'

'He's gone?' Wyeth queried.

'Well, I presume he has. He didn't come down this morning and his room is empty. Not that he brought much along with him, anyway.'

'Mind if I take a look?' Wyeth said.

'Why sure. But what interest would

you have in him?'

'None at all. I guess what my brother had to say just kinda got me intrigued.'

Magenta led the way up a flight of stairs and stopped outside an open door on the landing. 'Go right ahead,' she said.

Wyeth stepped into the room. There was a faint smell of tobacco and something else stale, but there was nothing to see. He walked across to the window and looked outside. The square was coming to life and round a corner down the main street he could just make out his brother's shop. Magenta had come in behind him.

'Did he say much?' Wyeth asked.

'I never spoke to him at all. He didn't spend much time in his room. He was out most of the time.'

'Thanks,' Wyeth said. Magenta looked at him with a slightly puzzled expression but he didn't want to be drawn into further discussion. He made his way down the stairs and took his farewell.

'Give my regards to your ma,' she said.

Wyeth walked away, thinking. His time with the cavalry and then on the run had taught him to be vigilant. He had developed something of a sixth sense, and it told him that there was something suspicious about the stranger. Whatever the man's business, it probably had nothing to do with him. It must only have been by chance that the stranger had been in his brother's shop. No one knew that Wyeth's real name was Holland. Still, it was wise to be cautious. It was only later, when he went to the livery stables and found his horse had gone, that he became really convinced.

He didn't waste any time. It was lucky that his mother had gone into town. It meant he didn't have to spend time explaining. Quickly, he hired a horse, returned for his guns and then rode out of town. There were a limited number of ways to go. Putting himself in the place of the horse thief, he figured out which was the most likely. He would want to get away quickly and find cover. That meant going the opposite way Wyeth had taken to get to the Barbed R. The trail was less marked and led away from the river towards the broken country known as the Brakes. He rode that way and was quickly rewarded by picking up the steeldust's sign. All his cavalry training came to his assistance and he knew his horse well; it was easy to trace her hoof prints. Too easy. Alongside them were prints made by another horse. Whoever had taken the steeldust was making no efforts to try and cover his tracks. Maybe he was just in too much of a hurry. But Wyeth suspected there was something more afoot.

As he rode he looked carefully about him. He was getting into the rougher country now. The ground was broken with thickets of mesquite and prickly pear and outcroppings of rock. It was more difficult to read the sign. The horse droppings, however, were relatively fresh. He had a feeling that he was getting closer to his target. He couldn't know for sure, but he had a pretty shrewd idea that he wasn't the victim of a simple case of horse theft. Whoever the stranger was, he was deliberately luring him on.

★   ★   ★

Gray had chosen his spot well. It was a place where the trail passed close to a tumbled pile of rocks. The natural assumption would be that anyone wishing to conceal himself would do so behind the rocks. On the other side of the trail, and a little way in advance, however, there was a thick patch of brush. Gray had hidden the horses well behind the rocks but had taken up position in the undergrowth. From there he had a clear, uninterrupted view of the trail. In his arms he cradled a Remington rolling block sporting rifle. It was single-shot but could be fired rapidly if needed. It was a weapon for buffalo hunters and sharpshooters. He prided himself on the latter appellation. His eyes swept the trail. He was well prepared for a long wait if necessary, but he didn't anticipate having to do so. It could be only a short time before Wyeth realized his horse was missing. If things worked out as he planned, Wyeth would be on his way already. He would ride straight into the trap prepared for him.

*   *   *

Wyeth was alert to danger. A man on the run didn't last long unless he developed a feeling for it. It was like it used to be in the war years, riding with Jeb Stuart, when survival often depended on having an instinctive eye for peril. It also often depended on being able to think like the enemy, to put oneself into the place of an opponent. So as he was riding, Wyeth was thinking: *What sort of place would*

I choose to bushwhack somebody? What sort of terrain would I be looking for? When he saw the rocky outcrop up ahead of him, he reasoned like Gray. That was the place someone would naturally choose to hide. But what about the patch of trees and brush opposite it? For someone to conceal himself there would be less expected. Furthermore, the stretch of ground between the bushes and the rocks was completely exposed — perfect for a back shot.

The trail took a slight dip. Taking advantage of it, Wyeth slid from the saddle and, hobbling his horse, slunk into the surrounding scrub. Keeping very low, he began to creep forwards, circling round the patch of brush as he did so. As he got nearer, he drew his pistol. Using all the craft he had learned while operating behind enemy lines, he inched forwards till he had a clear view of the area. He could see nothing so he shifted position. The change of angle brought him a first glimpse of his would-be assailant. It was an easy enough matter to slither forwards once more. The man was intent on watching the trail and did not hear a thing. When he was almost upon him, Wyeth stood upright.

'Don't move!' he snapped.

There was a brief instant before the stranger reacted. Twisting round, he raised his rifle and fired from the hip. Wyeth staggered back as the bullet sliced through the shoulder of his jacket. The stranger fired again and this time the bullet went whistling over Wyeth's head, thudding into a nearby tree and sending splinters of bark cascading into the air. Wyeth recovered his balance and, taking a moment to steady his hand, opened fire. There was no reaction from the man and Wyeth squeezed the trigger a second time. Still the man seemed unmoved till, all of a sudden, he toppled forward like a sawn log. Clutching at his shoulder, Wyeth stepped forward and turned the man over. His shirt front was soaked with blood from two bullet holes in his chest. Wyeth unfastened the man's bandanna, intending to try and stay the flow, but he quickly realized it was useless. The man's eyes stared unseeing. Wyeth took off his jacket and examined his own shoulder. He was lucky. The bullet had seared the flesh but nothing was broken.

He turned back to the dead man. Who was he? Why had he set the trap? Wyeth's first thought was that he must be a bounty hunter. When he felt inside the man's jacket and produced the Wanted notice, his conclusion seemed to be confirmed. He felt inside the man's other pockets. There wasn't anything unusual. He got to his feet and looked around for the man's horse. He couldn't see it and a brief look through the brush did not reveal it. He concluded that the stranger must have concealed his horse among the rocks further up the trail. Quickly, he moved back to where he had left his own horse and, climbing into the saddle with some little difficulty because of his shoulder, he rode the short distance to the rocks where he dismounted.

Sure enough, a brief search revealed the roan. It was restless at his approach but he quietened it down and then looked in the man's saddle-bags. Inside one of them was an envelope, sealed with the strange symbol of a tombstone on which was written *Cemetery Ridge*. He weighed it in his hand for a moment before tearing it open. Inside was a skull carved out of some black material resembling basalt. There was nothing more; no letter, nothing that might explain the mysterious image. His brow puckered. He had assumed that the man was a bounty hunter, that his motive had been merely mercenary. Now he wasn't so sure. The envelope and its contents were so odd that they had to be significant. They meant something.

His mind flew back to the time he had fought with Jeb Stuart at Gettysburg and that fateful second day. While

Pickett's charge to take Cemetery Ridge was underway, he had been locked in mortal combat on the right with the Federal cavalry of Brigadier Generals Gregg, Custer and Kilpatrick. He had been lucky to come away with his life. Pickett had gone down in legend, but the attack had failed. The next day the grey line began to plod its weary way through mud and drizzle, Stuart's cavalry guarding the left flank and rear of the retreating Rebels. They crossed the Potomac but the invasion of the North was defeated. The Army of Northern Virginia had made a valiant effort but the writing was on the wall. There were many twists and turns in the road after that, but the road led inexorably to Appomattox.

His face was grim as he recalled those days. But he had not surrendered. For him, the war continued. He put the skull back in the envelope and slipped the envelope into his pocket. He didn't know what it all signified, but he was certain now that the stranger's motive in seeking him out to kill him was not to claim any reward. There was something more to all this, something more sinister, which had to be connected with what had happened at Gettysburg. The stranger had failed in his mission, but somehow that word 'mission' summed up the situation. The man had been on a mission. He served some cause. And if that was the case, there must surely be others with the same mission, serving the same cause. As if it wasn't enough to have a bounty on his head, it seemed he was now also the target of some other group. When they got to know that he had survived, someone else would follow in the stranger's steps, seeking him out. Come to that; hadn't his brother mentioned seeing him talking with another man, another stranger, outside the Horseshoe saloon? There was probably nothing to that, but now more than ever he needed to exercise care.

One immediate consequence was that he couldn't go home again. To return to Winding would place his family in grave danger. He should never have gone back in the first place. Even without this complication, he had dreaded the act of taking his leave. It was better to just let it go. His mother, especially, would be upset, but there was really no alternative, no option but to move on. It was a lonely, dangerous trail he rode, but he had known that from the moment he had resolved to carry on fighting.

With fierce determination he climbed into the saddle. He sat for a few moments, undecided about which way to go; whether to carry on into the badlands or turn around and head for Cold Creek. To make for the badlands felt like a retreat. He quickly reached a decision. He turned the stranger's horse loose together with the one he had hired. Then, setting his spurs to the steeldust's flanks, he set his course for Cold Creek.

3

When the peace was signed at Appomattox Courthouse, most of the men who had been fighting on the Confederate side accepted, with greater or lesser reluctance, that they had lost and returned to their former lives. Others either could not or would not accept it. Wyeth and Rattlesnake were two of them. But there was a third group of people, who, while grudgingly accepting defeat, sought to place the blame on acts of treachery. For them the Union had not won the victory; elements of the Confederacy had lost it. One such man was Kirby Taylor.

A native of South Carolina, Taylor had done well out of the war, supplying the Confederate army with tents and blankets, boots and shoes. After the war, he was able to buy up land cheaply. The North had stipulated that all animals in the South should be requisitioned. Without horses, Southern farmers were unable to plough their land and reap a harvest. Faced with the problem of paying off their mortgages, they were forced to sell. Taylor had taken full advantage of the situation.

He had seen no active service, but when the war was over he liked to strike a pose. At such times he would maintain that the Confederate cause was not defeated, but merely subdued. He liked to associate with veterans, especially those still burning with resentment, and it was when he met some of these that he found a tangible target for his claim that the South had been betrayed from within. Gettysburg had been the decisive turning point of the war. Some of the men's resentment centred round their claim that the cavalry had delayed its arrival on the scene. If Jeb Stuart had turned up in time, the battle might have been won. It served his purpose to develop that theme, and it was only a short step from there to the formation of the Black Skull, a secret organization dedicated to avenging the supposed betrayal by hunting down and killing former members of the hard-riding horsemen in grey.

On the morning following his brief conversation with Hobbs, Taylor awoke to find that his secretary had already risen. He could smell the aroma of coffee and, presently, the sizzling of eggs and bacon. Quickly getting into his clothes, he strolled through to the living room of his well furbished mansion. Miss Hoskins appeared in the doorway leading to the kitchen.

'I hope you don't mind,' she said, 'but I figured you could probably do with a good breakfast after last night.'

Taylor grinned. 'I don't mind at all,' he said.

'I was just about to call you. It's almost ready. Take a seat at the table.'

Taylor pulled out a chair and sat down. Sunlight was falling into the room through the windows and when he glanced outside he had a view of a well-manicured lawn leading down to a tree-lined stream. It was a nice property. Life was good. Later, when he had enjoyed his breakfast — and Miss Hoskins — he would ride into town and wait for news of the stage. He was confident that things were about to get even better.

★　★　★

Wyeth had been riding steadily, putting ground between himself and the town of Winding. As he rode he had plenty of time to think about what had transpired, but he was no nearer arriving at a solution to the mystery of the envelope and its contents. He was feeling bad about leaving his family behind. He had considered turning round and going back to Winding, but had resisted the urge to do so. It wasn't right to do anything that might put them in danger. He thought about Jolie a lot. Maybe a day would come when they might be together, but he didn't see how.

On the evening of the second day he rode into a shallow stream and continued down it until he found a suitable place to make camp. He lifted the saddle from the steeldust and picketed the horse on a grassy slope. He built a fire and prepared a meal. It didn't amount to much because he was running low on supplies. When he had finished eating, he lay back with his head against his saddle. The night was chill and he leaned forward to throw a few branches on the dying embers of the fire. As it blazed up he thought he heard the sound of a footfall. Getting quickly to his feet, he drew his Colt .44 and stepped into the shadows.

In a few moments the bushes on the far side of the clearing parted and a figure emerged. He was outside the range of the flickering firelight and Wyeth couldn't discern anything clearly. The man was a vague shadow but as he stopped and glanced about,

Wyeth thought there was something vaguely familiar about him; that slight stoop, the set of the shoulders. The man moved forwards and as the light fell on him, with a jolt of surprise, Wyeth realized it was Rattlesnake Jack, the man he had been planning to meet in Cold Creek. Holstering his pistol, he stepped forwards. For a moment the man flinched and his right hand dropped involuntarily to his gun-belt. Then he recognized Wyeth.

'Gene,' he said. 'You made me start.'

'You're lucky I didn't shoot you. Didn't you realize the risk you were taking?' They paused to look more closely at each other and then they embraced.

'What the hell are you doin' here?' Wyeth said. 'I figured you were in Cold Creek.'

'I was,' Rattlesnake replied, 'but to tell you the truth, things are gettin' a mite uncomfortable back there. It wasn't long after you left that a posse of militia and cavalry showed up. There was a lot of activity. I figured the sensible thing might be for me to get out of town and at least try to warn you. You said you were visitin' your folks. It didn't take long to get on your trail.'

'Looks like those carpetbaggin' Yankee varmints are tryin' to clamp down on things. You did right to get away.'

'We need to think about where we go from here,' Rattlesnake said.

'Maybe drop out of sight for awhiles. I don't know. Maybe we should head for the Nations.'

Wyeth scratched his chin. 'I'd been wonderin' about that myself. It sure needs consideration. But right now ain't the time. Go get your horse. I'll build up the fire and put some fresh coffee on to boil.'

When they had drunk a few mugs of coffee and made themselves comfortable, Wyeth produced his pack of Bull Durham and they rolled smokes. Presently, the conversation returned to the immediate problem of what they should do next.

'Some of the boys have already gone to the Nations,' Rattlesnake said. 'We could maybe join forces with them.'

'I don't know,' Wyeth said. 'There's somethin' to be said for ridin' in a pack, but I prefer to do things differently.'

'Yeah, you've got a point. A couple of men working together can do a lot of damage behind enemy lines.'

'Yup, and that's just the situation we're in.' Wyeth blew smoke rings into the air. 'I've been thinkin',' he said. 'I got no argument against headin' for the Nations, but isn't that just what the Yankees would expect us to do? They might have stepped up things around Cold Creek, but I figure they'll be doin' exactly the same thing along the Missouri River.'

'I guess so.'

'No, I reckon we should do what we've done before, and aim for the place they won't be expectin' us.'

'And where's that?'

'Cold Creek, of course.'

'You were headin' that way already?'

'Yup. I guess I kinda got my mind fixed on that stagecoach caper. Sorry you've come all this way just to go back again, but that's the way I figure it.'

Rattlesnake grinned. 'Hell, I'm glad you said that, because that's the way I see it, too. I ain't been feelin' right since I left Cold Creek.'

'Appreciate you thinkin' of warnin' me,' Wyeth said.

From somewhere out in the night there came the sudden cry of a hoot owl. After a few moments they both broke into a laugh.

'I sure hope that means he's agreein' with us,' Rattlesnake said.

'I doubt it,' Wyeth replied. 'Ain't he supposed to be a wise old bird?'

★   ★   ★

The stagecoach line ran through Winding, Forestville, Oakchester, St Anthony and Towburg to Cold Creek. For several days, however, it had only carried passengers as far as Towburg. At the depot there it took on board an extra shotgun guard, while inside the stage, instead of passengers, four men armed with rifles took their places. They didn't ask questions. Although there didn't appear to be anything to guard, if Kirby Taylor, the new stage line owner, reckoned they were needed, that was his business. They were in his employ and he paid well. It was easy money, especially as they seemed to be getting paid for doing nothing. But if trouble turned up, they were ready for it.

★ ★ ★

Wyeth and Rattlesnake Jack sat their horses and looked down from a ridge on the stage route to Cold Creek. If they were right in their calculations and things went to plan, the stage should be coming through soon.

'I hope your informant's right about

that payroll,' Wyeth remarked.

'I ain't got any reason to doubt him. He works for the company.'

'You say he'd been talkin' about it in the saloon even before you got together with him? Seems to me he was bein' mighty indiscreet. I reckon the stage-coach company wouldn't be too pleased if they got to hear about it.'

Rattlesnake shrugged. 'I don't know. Maybe he'd had a drink too many. Maybe he was makin' it up.'

Wyeth looked out over the terrain. In the distance a faint cloud of dust indicated the approach of the stage. 'Well,' he said, 'let's hope he wasn't lyin'.'

'Hell, even if he was, we got nothin' to lose. If that stage ain't carryin' no payroll bullion, it's gonna be carryin' some Yankee double-dealers just waitin' to be relieved of their loot.'

'Yeah, loot that could be used to help some of their victims. Come on, what are we waitin' for?'

They rode down from the ridge and

concealed themselves behind a stand of timber by the side of the trail. The dust cloud grew bigger and when they could hear the clatter of hoofs they pulled up their bandannas so that only their eyes remained uncovered. They drew their pistols.

'Remember,' Wyeth said, 'We only use these if we have to. We're fightin' a different kind of war now.'

'You're too pernickety,' Rattlesnake replied.

The stage came into view. It was approaching a bend and as it slowed, Wyeth and Rattlesnake broke from cover. Wyeth raised his gun and fired into the air. Then, through the haze of dust, he caught his first sight of the driver and the two men riding with him on top of the stagecoach. Something was not right. He glanced quickly at Rattlesnake at the same moment that a blaze of gunfire broke out. Rattlesnake fell from the saddle as Wyeth's horse reared and pitched him to the ground. Bullets were tearing up the earth all around. Rattlesnake was bleeding from the chest but even from his prone position he was loosing off shots. There was no question now about the necessity of having to use their weapons. Wyeth fired at the stagecoach and then stooped down, seized the oldster by the collar and began to drag him back into the undergrowth.

They had chosen the spot well and they were soon screened by thick timber. Rattlesnake's horse had bolted but Wyeth's steeldust had come to a halt nearby. As quickly as he could, Wyeth dragged the oldster to his feet as bullets tore into the trees, showering them with branches and leaves.

'Are you hurt bad?' he asked. Rattlesnake grimaced. Without further ado, Wyeth sprang into the saddle. 'Here, take my hand and get up behind me,' he rapped. With Wyeth's strong arm supporting him, the oldster managed to drag himself up on to the steeldust's back.

'Hold tight on to me,' Wyeth yelled.

He dug in his spurs and the steeldust burst forwards at the same moment as the bushes parted and a group of the gunmen, who had been inside the coach, appeared with guns blazing. Most of their bullets thudded harmlessly into trees but one scorched across the horse's rump. The searing pain only served to make the animal gallop quicker. It was with difficulty that Wyeth managed to prevent her stampeding into the trees but a moment later she burst into the open and Wyeth knew that she couldn't be caught.

He flung a glance behind him. He could see the stagecoach standing by the trees at the side of the trail. The driver and one of the shotgun guards still remained at their places up top. Shots continued to be fired in the direction of the thundering steeldust, but they were out of range. Wyeth let the horse rush on. It seemed unlikely, but he couldn't be sure that they were safe from pursuit. Only when he was satisfied that they were finally clear did he slow the horse to a canter and then a trot. He turned his head to address Rattlesnake behind him.

'Are you holdin' up?' he asked.

The oldster muttered something, which Wyeth did not catch. He faced round and began to look for somewhere he could stop and tend to his friend. Ahead of him was a low hill with a cleft through which a stream flowed. He rode into it and after splashing through the water a little way, found a sheltered clump of oak and hickory. Drawing to a halt, he jumped from the saddle and then helped Rattlesnake to alight. He laid the oldster on the ground and then searched through his saddle-bags for his medicines. When he returned, Rattlesnake had passed out. It was just as well.

As gently as he could, Wyeth ripped the oldster's shirt aside. He had taken a bullet in the upper right chest. It was a nasty wound but it wasn't as bad as Wyeth had feared. The bullet had lodged just beneath the collarbone.

Wyeth took his knife, washed it in the stream and poured whiskey over it, and then dug into the bullet hole. He had acquired expertise during the war and it only took him a matter of moments to excavate the bullet. The oldster flinched and his eyes flickered but he did not wake. When Wyeth had finished he did the best he could to staunch the bleeding by stuffing the wound with his bandanna. He looked up. The steeldust was still sweating. He got to his feet and led it to the water. When the horse had drunk, he removed the saddle, gave it some grain and picketed it near the water. He built a fire and set about preparing some jerky broth. Then he waited for Rattlesnake to come round.

*　*　*

Although Jolie Rawley had learned not to be surprised by Wyeth's behaviour, it still hit her badly when she received the news of his sudden departure. She had come to town to do some shopping and stopped by his brother Shelby's store.

'Did he not say anything? Nothing about where he might have gone?'

'Nope. He didn't even say goodbye. We were expectin' him to stay a few days at least, but he just lit out without a word.'

'Your ma must be so upset,' Jolie replied, attempting to hide her own disappointment.

'Why not go over and pay her a visit? It'll do her good to see you.'

'Yes, I'll do that.'

When she got outside, she paused, holding on to a stanchion till she regained her composure. She looked up and down the street. Where she stood was in the shadow of an awning, but the street was bright with sunshine. People moved about; the scene was animated but it only made the pain she felt all the worse. She began to walk, occasionally nodding to an acquaintance. When she got as far as the square the door of the Willow House opened and Magenta Kirkwood appeared.

'Hello, Jolie,' she said.

Jolie halted and looked up. 'Oh, Magenta. Hello.'

'You seem to be preoccupied,' Magenta said.

'I'm sorry. It's true, I was miles away.'

'It must be nice to have Sam around. He stopped by here just the other day.'

Jolie looked at her with surprise. 'Sam was here?' she said.

'Yes. He was askin' about one of the boarders.'

'What did he say?'

'Why, nothing in particular. He seemed to be interested, though, because he took a look in the man's room. I don't think he found anything.'

'What man was this? Is he still staying with you?'

'Goodness, no. He'd already left before Sam showed up. In fact, the very same morning.' She paused. 'It was kinda unusual, I guess. Seems the man was in something of a hurry to be gone. Not that I'm complaining. Like I said to Sam, he paid his bill.'

Jolie did not reply. She seemed to Magenta to be even more preoccupied. 'Anyway,' she said, 'Give my regards to Sam when you see him.'

Jolie glanced up with a startled expression on her countenance. 'Sam isn't here,' she said. 'Apparently he's left town. I just found out myself.'

It was Magenta's turn to look surprised. 'What, gone already?'

'Yes,' Jolie said.

'His mother must be upset. Poor Lena.'

'I'm on my way to see her now,' Jolie replied.

'Make sure you let her know I was askin' after her.'

Jolie nodded and then resumed her way. She didn't notice the sunlight or the people or the general bustle. She was concerned only with what Magenta had told her. Was there some connection between Sam's sudden departure and the mysterious boarder? It seemed there must be, or why would Sam have been sufficiently interested in the stranger to pay a visit to the Willow House? But the main question that worried her was: Where had Sam gone? Maybe he had said something to his mother that might give her a clue. Because, without fully realizing it, she had already come to a decision. She was tired of waiting for Sam. Nothing had come of merely wishing and hoping. The time had come for her to do something about the situation and go to him.

* * *

Wyeth woke up with a start. He could only have been asleep for a matter of minutes or even less. Beside him, Rattlesnake Jack lay snoring. Wyeth had dressed the oldster's wounds with poultices, which he had tied with bandages made from an old shirt he had in his saddle-bags. Earlier, the oldster had spent a lot of time tossing and turning and thrashing about in his sleep, but now he seemed to be more comfortable. It looked like being a long night's vigil and Wyeth rolled and lit a cigarette. He knew that they were temporarily safe from pursuit, but he also knew that they couldn't afford to stay. It wouldn't be long before whoever was in the stagecoach would get on their trail, or the local marshal, or the cavalry, which Rattlesnake had reported as being active in the area. A wind had got up and the night was chill. He leaned over to adjust the oldster's blanket. As he did so, Rattlesnake's eyes flickered open and he looked into Wyeth's face.

'I ain't dead, then,' he said. 'Either that or there's some mighty ornery angels about.'

Wyeth grinned. If he was making jokes, it was a good sign that the oldster would pull through. 'How are you feelin' now?' he asked.

'Hurts like hell, but I'll be OK.'

'How about some coffee? I could put the pot back to boil.'

'I figure somethin' stronger might be in order.'

70

Wyeth handed Rattlesnake the flask containing the whiskey and the oldster took a long swallow. Then he took a few more. When he had almost drained the flask he attempted to sit up but fell back again.

'You know they'll come lookin' for us soon,' he muttered. Wyeth nodded. 'You don't have to stick around. There's no point in both of us stayin' here. You've done enough. I can take care of myself from here.'

'Shut up,' Wyeth said. 'I figure we should be safe for a day or two. After that we'll see what state you're in.' Rattlesnake didn't argue. He knew it was pointless. He looked up. A pre-dawn glimmer was lightening the sky.

'Gimme another little while,' he said, 'then if you give me a hand I can maybe get up in the saddle.' Wyeth didn't reply. 'Don't try and fool me,' Rattlesnake said. 'We both know we need to get out of here.'

They lapsed into silence till the

oldster spoke again. 'Where do you figure we should go? Head for the Nations, like we were thinkin'?'

Rattlesnake's suggestion made sense, but Wyeth wasn't sure that the oldster would make it that far. He needed a doc, and he needed one soon. There would be a doctor in Cold Creek, but he would be taking a huge risk going there. Wyeth's face was on a Wanted poster; the authorities would be looking out for him and Rattlesnake. It would be a foolish undertaking, but the more he thought about it, the more it seemed the only choice. He didn't like to admit it, but unless he got help soon, Rattlesnake's chances were thinner than a bone.

Before morning had dawned, Wyeth roused himself to water and feed the horse. When he had done so he lit a flame and heated the rest of the broth. The oldster had drifted into a troubled sleep again and Wyeth unwillingly shook him awake.

'Here, drink some of this,' he said.

He raised the oldster's head enough for him to ladle some of the broth into his mouth. Rattlesnake spluttered and broth ran over his grizzled chin.

'Hell,' he mumbled, 'what did you put in that?'

'It's an old recipe,' Wyeth replied. 'Got it from an old mountain man, 'cept you got jerky instead of bear.'

When Rattlesnake had finished, Wyeth set about removing all trace of the camp. Then he kneeled beside the oldster.

'Like you said last night, we gotta get you into the saddle.'

Rattlesnake did not demur. 'Try and put your arms around my neck. That's the way. Now brace yourself.'

Wyeth put his arms under Rattlesnake's armpits and, as gently as he could, hauled him upright. The oldster winced but otherwise did not give anything away. The horse was standing close by.

'OK, what's the best way of doin' this,' Wyeth muttered.

'Pity we ain't got but only the one hoss,' Rattlesnake said.

'There were plenty of times we got horses shot from under us when we were ridin' with Stuart,' Wyeth replied. Rattlesnake attempted a chortle but stiffened as a wave of pain swept through him.

'Sure were,' he said.

Wyeth's words seemed to encourage the oldster and with his assistance, he managed to place a foot in the stirrup.

'Ready?' Wyeth said.

'Ready.'

Rattlesnake's face twisted with the strain as he attempted to pull himself up. Wyeth pushed from below and with a mighty effort Rattlesnake hauled himself astride the steeldust. Wyeth climbed into the saddle.

'Hold tight, Rattlesnake,' he said. 'We ain't got far to go.'

'You'd do better just to leave me,' the oldster replied.

Wyeth ignored the comment. He touched his spurs to the horse's flanks and it stepped forwards.

Wyeth had some familiarity with the region and he had learned during his days as a guerrilla fighter to take note of every feature of a landscape and commit it to memory. Such knowledge was vital; it could mean all the difference between living and dying. He therefore avoided taking the direct route towards town. Instead, he followed a roundabout way, which would bring him by little-used trails that would offer the maximum of cover. As he rode his eyes searched the terrain, keenly alert to possible danger. To avoid the possibility of being dry gulched, he switched trails regularly. It wasn't something he seriously considered, but after his experience with the stranger in Winding he wasn't taking any chances. He needed to be cautious and at the same time make allowances for Rattlesnake's condition. He knew that every step must be causing the oldster pain but Rattlesnake gave no indication of it.

As they rode the light grew in

strength from moment to moment and the stars paled and vanished. Wyeth aimed to reach the town by mid-afternoon. He had considered whether to ride straight on in; the quicker Rattlesnake saw a doctor, the better it would be. On the other hand, to do so in broad daylight would only draw attention to them. They would be bound to arouse suspicion, sharing a horse. Rather than do that, he had decided that a better plan would be to leave Rattlesnake somewhere safe near town and then ride the rest of the way himself. That way he could carry out a reconnaissance of the place, search out the nearest doctor and then bring him back to treat the oldster. Just how he was going to do that was an open question. If the doctor could be persuaded to do so, all well and good. If not, he might just have to employ other means of encouragement.

4

Kirby Taylor's good mood did not last for long once he had driven Miss Hoskins back to Cold Creek and left her at her desk outside his private office. In the first place, the news from the stage depot was bad. His plan had succeeded in drawing not one but two robbers, either or both of whom could have been targets for the Black Skull, but they had both escaped. It was small consolation that one of them had been shot and wounded. With the sort of odds he had arranged in his favour, there should have been no chance of anyone getting away. Then, as if that weren't bad enough, he had been contacted later in the day by one of his operatives who had informed him that he had seen his fellow operative, Gray, being brought back dead to the town of Winding. Gray had been hot on the trail of Eugene Wyeth, one of Taylor's prime targets and a man he knew for sure had been with Jeb Stuart on that fateful day at Gettysburg. There was only one deduction to be drawn from that piece of information: Gray had been killed by Wyeth. He must have succeeded in tracking Wyeth down, but then things had gone badly wrong.

Taylor was sitting at a table in the Silver Diamond saloon with the operative who had brought him the news about Gray.

'Where is Wyeth now?' Taylor snapped.

The man shook his head. 'I don't know. I think I could recognize his picture from that Wanted dodger but he didn't show up in town. I waited around for a while till I finally figured the best thing was to get back to you pronto.'

'Couldn't you and Gray have teamed up? Two of you might have handled it better than one.'

'I suggested it, but Gray was keeping pretty tight about what he was doing. I figured he was still in Winding. He'd mentioned a spread called the Barbed R. Seems like he'd trailed Wyeth in that direction. I was thinkin' maybe I'd take a look. I was plumb amazed when I saw the marshal comin' down the street with Gray's body slung across a horse.'

'You're sure it was Gray?'

'Yeah. I was so surprised I made sure I got to take a closer look. It was Gray, all right. Seemed like he'd been shot in the chest. Pretty neat, too.'

Taylor helped himself to a drink from the bottle standing on the table. As he poured it down his throat, a thought occurred to him. Wyeth had somehow rumbled Gray and got away. Two men had tried to rob the stagecoach, which he had used as a decoy. Could Wyeth have been one of them? It wasn't an unreasonable assumption. If so, he was somewhere in the vicinity, in the company of his wounded companion. Who was he, and how badly was he injured? He finished the glass and poured another for himself and one for the other man.

'Tell me again, what's your name?' he said.

'Short,' the man replied. 'Zip Short.'

'Well, Mr Short,' he said, 'I don't need to remind you about our sacred cause.'

'No, sir,' Short replied.

'Then you'll appreciate how important it is that a skunk like Wyeth is hunted down and eliminated. Any man who did it would be doing the cause a huge service. I'd like to think that you're that man.' Short's chest seemed to visibly swell and a smile creased his otherwise hatchet features. 'Well, am I right?' Taylor continued. 'Do you have what it takes to be a hero for the old Confederacy?'

'Mr Taylor,' Short replied, 'I'm your man. I would take it as an honour to deal with Wyeth for you.'

'Not for me,' Taylor replied. 'For the cause.' He raised his glass and after a moment Short did likewise. 'To the

Confederacy,' Taylor said. They clinked glasses and drank. As they did so, Taylor took a sly look around to make sure no one was near enough to have heard their words. He had chosen a corner table deliberately but it was wise to be cautious.

'Get straight on the job,' Taylor said. 'I don't care a fig about the how or where or when. Just make sure Wyeth is eliminated. And I want to be kept informed about the whole situation. Report back to me when you have any news. Preferably when you've dealt with him. I hope I make myself clear.'

★　★　★

Wyeth drew the steeldust to a halt and dismounted. 'OK, Rattlesnake,' he said. 'I'm gonna help lift you down.'

The oldster didn't reply but gave a faint nod of the head. Supported by Wyeth, he half fell from the horse's back. Wyeth laid him on the ground in the shelter of some rocks. He propped the oldster's head up, wrapped him in a blanket and placed the whiskey flask and his pack of Bull Durham within easy reach.

'You're gonna be all right?' he said.

'Sure. I'll have me a regular hoe-dig while you're gone.'

'I'll be back real soon,' Wyeth said, 'with a doctor in tow.'

'Don't forget to find me a horse. I reckon I've got plumb familiar with your back.'

Wyeth swung into the saddle and moved off down towards Cold Creek. During the course of the ride they had not encountered anybody but now he rode with a renewed vigilance. The closer he got to town, the greater was the risk of running into trouble: from the law, from the cavalry, from some bounty hunter or a greenhorn out to make a name for himself. He was following an obscure, little-known trail, but that didn't guarantee there might not be a drygulcher hiding behind any rock or bush. He didn't think ahead too much about how he would proceed when he hit town. By then it would be dusk. That would help conceal his identity from anyone who might have seen his face on the Wanted poster.

The trail he was following petered out in some rough country cut by a few dry water courses. He continued riding till, coming round a bend, he began to pick up tracks left by other horses. Before long the town of Cold Creek came into view. Away to his right he caught a glimpse of the stagecoach trail. Lights were beginning to twinkle as he rode the remaining distance. He had been thinking hard but could come up with no better plan than to pay a visit to the Silver Diamond saloon and simply ask the barman where he might find a doctor.

He drew to a halt outside the saloon and dropped from the saddle. There were a number of horses at the hitch-rack and from inside the tinkling notes of a piano floated on the air. He stepped up onto the boardwalk and brushed aside the batwing doors. The atmosphere was heavy with smoke and the stale smell of beer-stained sawdust. Nobody paid him much attention as he strode to the bar. The barman looked up at his approach.

'Whiskey,' he said.

There were a few men standing together at the bar. They carried on talking without a break and it was only when he glanced up at the mirror that Wyeth observed one man sitting at a table, who seemed to be looking a little too closely in his direction. He might not have noticed him except for the fact that he was wearing quite a distinctive checked shirt. As Wyeth's attention fell on him, his eyes dropped and he reached out for the glass standing at his elbow. Wyeth threw back the whiskey and then ordered another. As the bartender was pouring the drink, Wyeth leaned forward.

'Say,' he remarked, 'you wouldn't know where I can find a doctor?'

The barman regarded him frankly. 'Sure,' he said. 'There's Doc Shuman. He's mainly a horse doctor but he doubles up as a quack. Just turn left and keep walkin'. You'll see his shingle right next to the livery stables.'

Wyeth nodded. 'Thanks,' he said. It was as easy as that. No questions asked. Knocking back his drink, he turned and began to make his way outside. A woman approached him and he was temporarily distracted. Only when he reached the batwings did he remember to look back. The man who had been looking at him was no longer sitting at his table. Wyeth had not seen him get up or go out. Without thinking much of it, he walked out into the gathering dusk.

It didn't take him long to find the livery stables but he could see no sign of the doctor's shingle. He didn't need to. There was a man sitting on a tilted-up seat outside the livery.

'Know where I can find Doc Shuman?' Wyeth asked.

'I'm Shuman. I don't know about any doc.'

'The bartender at the Silver Diamond told me you do some doctorin'. Is that right?'

The man didn't look like Wyeth's idea of a doctor. He was unkempt and the clothes he was wearing were ragged. A flicker of a smile seemed to pass across his face as if he found Wyeth's words amusing.

'I expect he told you to look out for my shingle,' he said. Wyeth did not respond. 'Figure I could turn my hand to some doctorin',' the man resumed, 'but I ain't no regular sawbones.' Wyeth hesitated, not sure what to make of the situation.

'What's your problem?' Shuman said. 'You look fit enough to me.'

'It ain't me that needs a doc. It's a friend.'

The man's eyes were keen and they scrutinized Wyeth closely. 'So is there some kinda reason you gotta fetch somebody? Rather than bring him, I mean.'

'He's been shot,' Wyeth said. 'I dug out the bullet but he ain't lookin' so good.'

'Where'd he get hit?'

'In the chest.'

'Where did you leave him?'

'A few miles outa town.'

The man continued to look at Wyeth. 'Give me a minute,' he said. 'I'll get my horse and medicine bag.'

He got to his feet and as he made to enter the livery stables Wyeth suddenly remembered that he needed a mount for Rattlesnake.

'I need to hire a horse,' he said.

'OK,' the man replied. 'Come right on in and you can pick one out.'

'What, you're the ostler, too?'

The man grinned. 'Ostler, blacksmith, horse dealer; you name it.' Wyeth noticed he didn't include doctor on his list.

In no time at all, Wyeth and Shuman were riding out of town. Wyeth had chosen a chestnut gelding for Rattlesnake. It wasn't much of a horse but it would have to do. They hadn't gone far when Shuman rode up close.

'Just as a by the way,' he said, 'I figure I know who you are.'

Wyeth did not show surprise. 'Yeah?' he replied.

'Your picture's all around town. You were takin' some risk showin' yourself in Cold Creek.'

'Not as much risk as you're taking ridin' along with me,' Wyeth responded.

The man chortled and spat. 'It's fine by me,' he said. 'I don't hold no candle for the Union. You and me, we're on the same side. Then and now.'

Night had fallen but Wyeth had no difficulty locating Rattlesnake. The oldster was lying just as he had left him except that in his right hand he held a .44 instead of the whiskey flask.

'You forgot the signal,' he said.

Wyeth grinned. 'Seems to me you're makin' a recovery,' he said. 'Guess I brought the doc all the way out here for nothin'.'

Rattlesnake grunted and looked up at

Shuman. 'Nice of you to take the time,' he said.

Shuman lifted down his bag and kneeled beside the oldster. From the bag he produced a pair of scissors with which he proceeded to cut Rattlesnake's shirt and then the makeshift bandage. When he had done so, he peered closely at the wound. Wyeth, leaning over, could see that the flesh around the wound seemed to have turned a shade of blue.

'The wound is infected,' Shuman said, 'but it ain't too bad.' He looked up at Wyeth. 'It's lucky you found me. Put some water on to boil.'

Wyeth built a fire and placed the blackened kettle over it. When the water had boiled Shuman set about cleaning Rattlesnake's wound. His touch was surprisingly gentle, but even so the oldster flinched. Once he had cleaned the wound Shuman began to pack something around it.

'What's that you got there?' Wyeth asked.

'Salt pork. Nothin' better that I know of. Here, take some of this and boil it up.' He observed Wyeth's puzzled expression. 'Comfrey leaves. Knitbone. Good for inflammation.'

When Wyeth had carried out his instructions, he applied the mass of hot greenery to the infected area and finally bandaged it all up.

'There, that should hold it,' he said to Rattlesnake. 'How do you feel?'

'I'll be fine. How about some coffee?' the oldster replied. Wyeth set about making it the way he knew Rattlesnake liked it: black, muddy and strong.

★　★　★

The stagecoach pulled into the depot at Cold Creek and Jolie Rawley stepped from it. She stopped for a moment to look up and down the street. During the course of the journey from Winding she had been troubled by a bad conscience, but now that she had arrived at her destination she felt her spirits lift. Although the only information she had was what Wyeth's mother had told her, she felt a renewed confidence that she would find him in Cold Creek. After all, it wasn't such a huge place. She waited for her bag to be lifted down and then set off up the street to find the Commodore Hotel. Although it failed to live up to its title, it was not hard to find. She booked a room and was shown to it by the desk clerk.

'I hope you will find this satisfactory,' he said as he opened the door.

Jolie swept inside. Her first impressions were good. The room was quite well furnished and it looked clean and tidy.

'Thank you,' she said. 'This will be fine.'

The clerk placed her bag on a chair. 'Just contact me if there's anything you need,' he said.

When he had gone she sat down on the bed and let out a deep sigh. She had glanced in the hotel registry on the off chance that she might see Sam Holland's name, but it wasn't there. She was not in the least discouraged; she hadn't expected it to be. Her confidence that she would find him remained high. She hadn't given very much thought to what might happen after that. Once she had taken the decision to find Wyeth, she had been too occupied with simply getting to Cold Creek. She hadn't liked leaving her father behind; to avoid unnecessary and complicated explanations, she had told him she was visiting a friend for a few days.

Eventually, she got to her feet and walked to the window. Her room overlooked the main street. Things seemed relatively quiet. Maybe that was why her eye was drawn to a man who stood on an opposite corner, leaning against a stanchion. He was in the process of lighting a cigarette and when he had done so he looked up in her direction. Something made her move back. When she looked again he was still there, looking towards the hotel. He remained that way for a minute or two and then turned on his heel and began to walk away. She watched him till eventually he turned in at the Silver Dollar saloon then she began to unpack the few items she had brought with her.

★   ★   ★

The morning following his treatment at the hands of Shuman, Rattlesnake felt a lot better. After eating breakfast, he and Wyeth sat talking with the would-be doc.

'You know,' Shuman said, 'you boys ought to go easy.'

'Yeah, we will, at least till Rattlesnake's recovered.'

'I don't mean that. I mean there's a lot of Federal cavalry about. Things could get mighty hot for folks such as yourselves.'

'Thanks for the warning,' Rattlesnake replied. 'I already noticed that for myself. I was halfway to the Nations before Wyeth here persuaded me to head for Cold Creek.'

'You could do worse. What made you decide on Cold Creek?'

'We had plans,' Wyeth replied.

'Let me take a guess,' Shuman said. 'Would these plans have somethin' to do with robbin' the stagecoach?'

Wyeth and Rattlesnake exchanged glances. 'What makes you think that?' Wyeth said.

Shuman chuckled. 'Hell,' he said, 'there's been so many rumours about that payroll, I figured there had to be somethin' more to it.'

'What do you mean?'

'Look, I don't have to spell it out. I reckon what happened to Rattlesnake here tells its own tale.'

'You weren't wrong to be suspicious about that payroll story,' Wyeth said. 'Sure, we figured to take the payroll. It was a setup; the stage was full of armed guards.'

Shuman thought for a few moments. 'Let me give you boys a word of advice,' he said. 'I don't suppose you ever heard the name Kirby Taylor?'

Wyeth shook his head but Rattlesnake showed interest. 'Sure, I heard of him,' he said. 'Ain't he some sort of big shot around Cold Creek?'

'Yeah, that's him. Amongst other things, he owns the stage company. I ain't got much to go on, but to my way of thinkin' it was Taylor who authorized those rumours. I don't know why. Put it down to the fact that there's somethin' about the varmint I just don't like. I could show you other folks who feel the same way. Some of them have been on the wrong end of Taylor's methods.'

'His 'methods'?' Wyeth queried.

'Oh, don't get me wrong. There ain't anythin' much you could put your finger on; he stays within the law. But all the same, he makes sure he gets what he wants.'

'If you're right, and this *hombre* Taylor is behind what happened to us, I swear I'm gonna get even,' Rattlesnake snarled.

'Well, you're not in any position to be doin' anything just yet,' Shuman said. He turned to Wyeth. 'What do you and Rattlesnake figure to do now?' he asked.

'Lie low till Rattlesnake's fit to ride.'

'That sounds reasonable, but where do you folks intend on stayin'?'

'Right here,' Wyeth said.

Shuman shook his head. 'Too dangerous,' he replied, 'what with those cavalry men around. The law will be lookin' for you, too. Rattlesnake ain't exactly in the best condition to be roughin' it. You need somewhere to lie low. Why don't you stay with me till Rattlesnake's better? It shouldn't take too long. I got room at the livery stables. Allowin' that we don't make any fuss about ridin' into town, there's no reason anyone would suspect you were there.'

Wyeth looked at Rattlesnake. 'Hell,' the oldster said, 'I'm fit to ride now. Just hoist me up on to that old chestnut.'

'You might be able to ride, but you're

in no condition to be ridin' far.'

'You're sure about this?' Wyeth said to Shuman. 'You could be landin' yourself in a heap of trouble shelterin' an outlaw.'

'Be glad of your company,' Shuman replied. 'Like I said, I ain't no friend of the Yankees. You, Rattlesnake and me, we fought on the same side. I ain't sayin' as I think you boys are wise to be carryin' on the war, but if it comes to a choice, you sure got my support. Especially at a time like this.'

'We appreciate it,' Wyeth said. He turned to Rattlesnake. 'Shuman's right. You're not in a state to be ridin' hard. I figure we should take up his offer.'

'You're very welcome,' Shuman said.

'We won't forget this,' Wyeth replied.

Shuman shrugged. 'Then it's settled,' he said. 'I reckon we'd be OK simply ridin' into town, but there's some woods right behind the livery stables. We could go that way.'

'Sounds good,' Wyeth said. 'We'll finish up here and then move.'

5

Shuman had been right to warn Wyeth and Rattlesnake about the presence of Federal cavalrymen in the area. They had barely started out for Cold Creek when they heard the drumming of hoofs.

'How many of 'em?' Shuman asked.

Wyeth listened closely. 'About a dozen,' he said, and Rattlesnake nodded in agreement. 'Soldiers,' he said.

They looked about. A little way off was a grove of trees. Applying their spurs, they rode into shelter. The drumming of hoofs grew louder. Soon they could hear the creak of saddle leather and then a body of horsemen came into view. Rattlesnake was correct. It was a group of cavalrymen, their blue uniforms showing sharp and crisp against the skyline. The trail they were following cut across that which Shuman had chosen and the riders cantered past within a matter of yards. When the last of them had vanished from sight, Wyeth led the others out from cover.

'Better take a different trail,' he said. He led them in the direction he had followed on his previous visit to town. After the incident with the soldiers, they were even more alert to possible danger, but it had also set Wyeth's brain to thinking along a new track. Presently he rode up close to Rattlesnake.

'I figure you weren't just blowin' off hot air when you said you wanted to get even with those varmints who shot you,' he said.

Rattlesnake glanced at him. 'If I know you, I figure you feel the same way, too.'

Wyeth grinned. 'Well,' he said, 'I just had an idea. Seems like we fell for that story about the Federal payroll. But the fact remains there's a lot of soldiers garrisoned round here and they need to be paid. That's what made the story convincin'. So, where is the money to pay them?'

Rattlesnake thought for a moment. 'I don't know. In the bank, I guess.'

'Yeah, that's the way I figure it. No matter which way that money gets here, it's got to be kept in the Cold Creek bank.'

Rattlesnake nodded. 'I think I catch your drift,' he said.

'Yeah. This is what I been thinkin'. We got a place to stay. While you carry on makin' a recovery, why don't I take the opportunity to take a look at the bank, see how things operate? Then when you're ready, we could see about relievin' the bank and the cavalry of their funds.'

Rattlesnake nodded his head in the direction of Shuman, who was riding just ahead of them. 'What about him?' he asked.

'What about him?' Wyeth replied.

'Do we cut him in on the plan?'

Wyeth thought for a moment. 'I don't know,' he replied. 'Maybe it depends on just how he's fixed. Let's see how it goes.'

* * *

Zip Short could hardly believe his luck. Following his conversation with Kirby Taylor, he had almost immediately run into Wyeth. He hadn't needed to make any effort to find his target. Wyeth had simply walked into the Silver Dollar saloon. It was almost too good to be true. He had slipped away, thinking that he might even be able to backshoot Wyeth when he emerged from the saloon. That had not proved possible. When Wyeth emerged he had made his way down the main street only as far as the livery stables. From the shelter of a nearby alley, Short had watched as Wyeth engaged in conversation with the ostler. When they rode out together a little while later, he had been tempted to follow but had not done so. It would take time to get his horse, but more importantly, he had made the decision to go about things more methodically. He would wait his time. At some point, Wyeth would return. Even if he didn't, Short had little doubt that he would be able to elicit any information he wanted from the ostler. All he had to do was to keep his eye on the livery stables. Short wasn't an especially thoughtful individual, but there were certain things about the situation which struck even him as slightly odd. What was Wyeth's business with the ostler? Why had they left town so suddenly at a comparatively late hour? Maybe there was something here that would work to his benefit.

Short's luck held. He had been prepared to wait indefinitely for the reappearance of Wyeth, but quite early on the day after he had seen him riding out of town in the company of the ostler, he was rewarded by the sight of them riding back again. They had chosen to arrive at the livery stables by way of the woods at the back, but he had been prepared for that. The only thing that puzzled him was why there were now three riders instead of two. It was something to think about, but even more than that, he had a sense that it was the kind of information that Kirby Taylor would be interested in knowing. Once he had eliminated Wyeth, of course. Wyeth remained his prime target. He reached into the pocket of his jacket and fingered the little black carved skull. Wyeth might have survived Gray's assassination attempt, but he wouldn't escape this time.

★ ★ ★

Kirby Taylor had rapidly grown tired of Miss Hoskins. So when he observed a new lady in town, he was immediately interested. It wasn't often that Cold Creek received a visit from such a fresh and beautiful young woman. He had observed her alight from one of his stagecoaches while looking down from his office window and had immediately summoned one of his employees to follow her and observe where she went.

When the time was ripe he would introduce himself to her. Apart from the natural interest she aroused in him, he was intrigued. What would somebody like her be doing in town? The question added a dash of piquancy to the prospect of meeting her.

Moving to the door, he opened it and crossed the outer reception area, ignoring his secretary and sweeping past before she could open her mouth to say anything. Once outside, he made his way to the stage depot. The horses had been unhitched and the stagecoach stood in the yard. With a glance in its direction, Taylor opened the door of the office. A railing divided the room and he pushed through it. Hobbs, the clerk, was sitting behind his desk writing something on a piece of paper. He looked up apprehensively at Taylor's arrival.

'Good day, Mr Hobbs,' Taylor announced.

'Good day,' Hobbs muttered.

Taylor's eye swept the room before

fastening on the agitated clerk. 'No problems with the latest run?' he asked.

'No, sir. On time as usual.'

'There was a young lady among the passengers. Take a look at your schedules and see where she got on.'

Hobbs knew better than to ask any questions. He searched among some papers and then looked up.

'Winding,' he replied.

Taylor was thoughtful. 'Winding,' he reiterated. 'Seems like I've heard that name before.'

'It's been a regular stop for some time.'

'I don't mean that,' Taylor snapped. 'I mean recently.'

Hobbs relapsed into silence. He was relieved when, a few moments later, Taylor turned and made his exit without any further comment. Once outside, Taylor paused and then began walking again. He had remembered where he'd heard the name of Winding. Nothing to it, of course, but it was something of a coincidence that it happened to be the name of the same town Short had mentioned; the town to which his agent Gray had tracked Wyeth before coming to a sticky end.

Shuman's offer of a place to stay proved to be the loft above the livery stables. Apart from the aroma of horse flesh and dung, it was quite habitable. Shuman had installed a few amenities, chief among which were a bunk bed, a table and a couple of chairs. Rattlesnake took the bunk. Wyeth was content to make his bed of straw.

'I agree it ain't quite the Commodore Hotel,' Shuman said, 'but I guess you could make yourselves comfortable.'

'It's fine,' Wyeth said. He didn't bother to ask about the Commodore. He was anxious to take a closer look at the town but he knew he would be taking a big risk.

'What you need is some sort of disguise,' Shuman said.

Wyeth took a look at himself in a broken mirror hanging from a nail on the wall. Since meeting up with one another, both he and Rattlesnake had a growth of beard.

'I don't figure anyone would recognize me from that Wanted dodger,' he said. 'It wasn't much of a likeness to begin with.'

Shuman took a look at him. 'Yeah,' he said, 'I guess you're right. Just be careful what you're doin'.'

Wyeth stepped out into the open. The livery stables were situated towards one end of the main street and the bank was at the other. He began to walk in its direction, passing the Commodore Hotel and the Silver Dollar saloon. Between him and the bank stood the marshal's office. A Wanted poster with his name on it was stuck to the wall outside and Wyeth glanced at it as he passed. It was probably true that no one would be likely to recognize him from a casual observation. He carried on walking till he came to the bank and after a moment's hesitation, walked inside. The place was quite busy; while the cashier was dealing with the line of customers he had time to take a good look at the layout of the place. There was only one cashier on duty but behind the counter and grill there was a door leading to another room. As he watched the door opened and a second man emerged. He threw a comment over his shoulder to someone, who was obviously in the room, and then took his seat beside the other cashier. Wyeth had seen enough. Turning on his heel, he went back outside and began to make his way towards the stage depot. He and Rattlesnake had been victims of a setup. Maybe he could discover a bit more about who and what was involved.

★ ★ ★

Jolie Rawley came down for breakfast on the day following her arrival. The dining room was quiet, with only two other tables occupied. At one sat a weary-looking man of indeterminate age, who looked like some sort of drummer, and at another sat a middle-aged couple. As she ate another man entered the room and, to her surprise, approached her table.

'Excuse me, ma'am, but would you mind if I joined you?'

She looked at him. He was well dressed in a dark brown suit with a silk shirt and string tie. A dark shadow lined his jaw but he had obviously taken time with his toilette and smelled of some kind of cologne. Before she could reply to his query, he had taken a seat opposite her.

'I trust that you have found everything to your satisfaction so far,' he said. 'I'm the owner of the hotel.'

A waitress approached the table. 'Is there anything else you would like?' Taylor asked.

'No, I'm fine,' Jolie replied. Taylor looked up at the girl.

'More coffee,' he said. He turned back to Jolie. 'I hope you won't find me forward,' he said, 'but I assume you're new to our little town. I know how disconcerting it can be until you get to know a place. I wouldn't like you to get a bad impression, so if there's anything I can do to make your stay more pleasant, please just let me know. I have some influence.'

Jolie felt slightly more relaxed. 'Thank you,' she said. 'That's very kind.'

'I wouldn't say Cold Creek has an awful lot to offer, but it has its points of interest.'

Jolie was thinking. She had come to Cold Creek to find Wyeth. Maybe she had struck lucky. If anyone was likely to have heard anything of him, it was this man. He seemed to be the sort of person who would have his hand on the pulse of what was going on in town and he was obviously influential.

'Allow me to introduce myself,' the man was saying. 'My name is Taylor, Kirby Taylor.' His words seemed to hang in the air and on his face there was a look of anticipation.

'Rawley,' she replied, 'Jolie Rawley.'

'Very nice to make your acquaintance,' he said.

* ★ *

Zip Short was ready. He had observed Wyeth as he emerged from the livery stables and made his way into town. Assuming Wyeth would come back the same way, he had taken up position in an alleyway on the opposite side of the street. There was a chance that Wyeth would return via the back of the stable, but Short didn't think it likely. The alleyway led from the main drag to a maze of narrow streets behind and running parallel to the livery. He had no doubts about being able to make a getaway. Occasionally, people approached but when they did he just slipped back into the shadows. Once, the light at the end of the alley had darkened and a man had advanced part of the way along it before apparently changing his mind and going back again. He had a clear view of the livery stables from his position. He wet his lips and drew his gun. He hefted it in his hand for a few moments before slipping it back into its holster. Then he leaned forward so he could see down the street.

No sign of Wyeth as yet. He put his hand inside his jacket and felt the black skull. He began to figure out how he would leave the black skull as a memento on Wyeth's dead body. It was a problem. Once he had carried out the execution, he would need to escape the scene as quickly as possible. He considered the matter further till it became a preoccupation. He began to obsess about how to place the black skull on Wyeth's corpse, as if that was what really mattered. It was only when he heard a sound behind him that he was jerked back into reality. He turned round, expecting to see someone, but there was nobody. There came another scuffling sound and he looked down to see a lean-looking cat inching its way towards him. For a second his hand stole towards his gun and then he came to his senses and simply took a threatening step towards it. The cat slunk by him and ran out into the main street. He spat after it and then, this time drawing his gun, turned towards the street himself.

★　★　★

Wyeth's visit to the stage depot had not initially been successful. On the pretext of making inquiries about buying a ticket, he had spoken with the clerk, a weedy individual, but had been unable to draw him out. To ask anything too directly would have been to arouse suspicion. As he emerged from the depot, however, he saw a coach standing in the yard and stopped to take a look at it. There was nothing unusual about it; it was just another slightly worn and battered Concord. He leaned forward to glance in the window and saw something dark outlined against the upholstery of the bench seat. He tried the door handle and it opened. He reached inside and picked up the object. It was a black basalt skull. It must have fallen from someone's pocket, and since he had come across something similar before, he knew that it could have been no ordinary passenger. It must have belonged to one of the gunmen who had occupied the coach and shot Rattlesnake. It was fair to assume, too, that the occupants on that occasion had not been soldiers. Pocketing the skull, he turned and began to make his way back in the direction of the livery stables.

After his discovery of the skull, he was more alert than ever. The man who had tried to kill him had possessed such a skull. It wasn't just a question now of someone possibly recognizing him from the Wanted poster. He was in even greater peril than he had imagined. He had been a guerrilla, fighting at times behind enemy lines, and he was trained to spot danger. He didn't even need that experience to notice the alleyway on the opposite side of the street, a little way beyond the livery stables. He had turned in the opposite direction when he started out. As he looked towards it, a cat suddenly spurted out. Wyeth's reactions were instantaneous as he ducked and began to run. He knew what he had to do, and that was to avoid trouble. If he got involved in anything, it would blow his cover. Seeing a shop doorway, he ran inside as a shot rang out, rapidly followed by another. A bell rang and he paused a moment to look around. He was in some sort of ladies' clothing store. An elderly woman was trying on a hat. She looked up with a startled expression.

'Sorry, ma'am,' he said. The store-keeper began to say something but Wyeth interrupted him. 'Is there a back way out of here?'

The man seemed too dazed to reply but instead pointed down the room towards a curtained recess. Without waiting for the storekeeper to find his tongue, Wyeth vaulted over the counter. The woman screamed as Wyeth ripped aside the curtain. In a flash he realized his mistake. The curtain did not lead to another room but screened a changing room. A second woman, scantily clad, was inside. She did not scream like the first lady but merely looked at him with a blank expression.

'My mistake,' Wyeth snapped. He noticed for the first time that there was a second door behind the salesman. He flung it open. It led into a storeroom with an outer door in the corner. It was standing partly open and he ran through it. Somewhere in the background he heard the report of a gun and the crash of broken glass but he had already cleared a fence and was hurtling down a narrow street of residential properties. He came to a fork and took another street, which led him further away from the centre of town. He slowed down as the houses petered out and he saw trees ahead. He realized it was the same grove of trees that backed on to the livery stables. Once within their shelter he knew he was safe.

He stopped to recover his breath, regretting that he had not been able to fight it out with his assailant. He knew who would have come out on top in a shootout, but it was something he couldn't afford to happen. One thing was true: the beard had not served as a disguise. The man who had taken those shots had recognized him. That gave him a big advantage; Wyeth did not know who the man was, but he knew Wyeth. Every time Wyeth stepped outside the confines of the livery stables, he would be putting himself in the firing line. Any doorway, any open window, any alleyway could conceal his would-be killer. He could strike at any time. Maybe Shuman's idea about a disguise wasn't so absurd after all. Thinking this way, he started to grin when he recalled his unwanted arrival in the changing room — that was a second opinion the woman had certainly not been expecting.

*   *   *

Evening came. The air was warm and Wyeth and Shuman sat outside. A bottle of whiskey stood on a table and Shuman poured drinks into two glasses.

'Here's to you,' Wyeth said. 'Me and Rattlesnake sure owe you.'

'Rattlesnake seems to be makin' a good recovery,' Shuman replied. 'When I changed his dressings earlier, the wound looked like it's healin' good.' He paused. 'Say, why do you call him Rattlesnake?'

Wyeth laughed. 'I guess you must have noticed that two fingers of his left hand are missin'. Seems like he chopped them off himself with an axe after gettin' bit by a rattlesnake.'

'Well, then I ain't too surprised he's on the mend. What's a bullet in the chest after that?'

'It was before I met him. It might be

a story for all I know. The fact remains, I don't reckon Rattlesnake would have pulled through without you.'

Shuman did not reply. The wind soughed through the leaves, carrying the sounds of the horses in the corrals. Wyeth thought through the day's events.

'I took a walk down to the stage depot,' he said after a while.

'Yeah? That used to be a nice little operation till Kirby Taylor took it over.'

'Kirby Taylor? The man you mentioned before?'

'Yeah. The stage line is just one of his businesses. Seems like he owns half the town and a lot of land besides. I should know. Some of it was once mine.'

'He owns a parcel of land?'

'He's got a finger in a lot of pies, but his main property is a place he calls the Valhalla. And he don't take kindly to visitors.'

'What does he do with it? Farm? Run cattle?'

'He don't do nothin' with it so far as

I can see. I guess he just likes to look at it. A mighty pretty spot, too. The river runs right through it.'

Wyeth was thoughtful. He reached into his pocket and produced the two black skulls. 'Do you make anythin' of those?' he asked.

Shuman took the carvings and looked closely at them. 'Where did you get them?' he asked.

'One of 'em was in the possession of a man who tried to bushwhack me. I found the other on the seat of one of Taylor's stagecoaches.'

'I ain't seen anythin' like these before,' Shuman said. 'What do you think?'

'I'm danged if I know, but I aim to find out.'

'How are you goin' to do that?'

Briefly, Wyeth told Shuman what had happened on the way back from the stage depot. 'There's got to be some kinda connection,' he said. 'These things are tied in somehow and I figure that skunk who took those shots at me knows the answer.'

'You'd better watch yourself if he knows who you are. Maybe he's just another galoot out for the reward.'

'Maybe, but I doubt that's the reason he's gunnin' for me.' He pondered for a few moments. 'From what you've said, I figure Kirby Taylor must be involved. I was thinkin' of tryin' to flush out the varmint who took those shots, but it might be a better idea to pay a visit to Valhalla.'

Shuman gave him a quizzical look. 'You ain't plannin' on doin' anythin' foolish?' he asked.

Wyeth suddenly grinned. 'Well,' he said, 'as a matter of fact you could say I'm aimin' to do just that; and I'm not referrin' to Kirby Taylor.' He paused to knock back the last of the whiskey in his glass before pouring himself and Shuman another. 'The thing is,' he resumed, 'Rattlesnake and me are fixin' to relieve the bank of all its cash before we're finished.'

Shuman looked hard at Wyeth. His

expression was one of incomprehension. Then suddenly his puckered brows straightened and, flinging himself back in his chair, he began to laugh.

'Hell,' he said, 'you boys really don't believe the war is over.'

'You won't be involved,' Wyeth said. 'We don't want to get you into trouble.'

'What if I want to be involved?' Shuman replied. 'Hell, this is gettin' to be fun. I ain't had a time like this in years. I'm sure glad you turned up. Just say I'm in, that's all.'

It was Wyeth's turn to look hard at his companion. In a moment his face began to crack and he broke into a laugh, too. When they had quietened down, Shuman sat up straight and raised his glass.

'To the Confederacy,' he said.

Wyeth raised his own glass. 'To Robert E. Lee and the Army of Northern Virginia,' he replied.

6

Kirby Taylor drew the buckskin he was riding alongside Jolie Rawley to a halt. He had chosen a particularly scenic spot overlooking a long stretch of the river with which to impress her.

'There,' he said. 'As good a view as you'll find in the entire state.'

'It really is beautiful,' Jolie responded.

'Come on,' he said, 'why don't we stretch our legs.'

He got down from the horse and then walked round to Jolie's side to help her dismount but she forestalled him and had already taken a step away before he could take her arm. They began to meander down the path, a little way along which was a stand of trees. As they came to the end of the wooded stretch Jolie had her first view of the house. It was bigger than she had expected from what Taylor had told her.

It consisted of two storeys with a flat roof. Ornate Greek columns flanked an impressive main entrance but what was equally striking was a tall single chimney which rose above the centre of the roof like a column. A long manicured lawn led down to the river.

'It's built in a style familiar to all Virginians,' Taylor said, standing alongside her.

'It's a lovely house,' Jolie replied.

'It's very well situated,' Taylor replied. 'The covered bridge you see in the distance is the only way across the river for some miles. I can't say that I'm responsible for choosing the location, but it certainly influenced my decision to buy it and make it my home.'

'You like to be private?' Jolie asked.

'I'm a very busy man. My time is taken up with all manner of concerns. When I'm not working, it's very important to me to be able to relax amid pleasant surroundings. I need to have space.'

'I know what you mean. My father

owns a ranch. I don't think I could well endure to live in the confines of a town.'

'You do not, then, live in Winding?'

As soon as he had said the words he knew he had made a tactical mistake. She looked up at him sharply.

'How do you know where I come from?'

'You forget that I'm the owner of the stage line. I was merely making an assumption. An unwarrantable one, I agree. I hope you will forgive me.'

His look was so contrite that she forgot her momentary flash of annoyance. 'You have no need to apologize,' she said. 'Yes, you are right. My father owns a ranch near to the town. It's called the Barbed R.'

Something registered in Taylor's memory, but he couldn't quite locate it. He was suddenly a lot more interested. 'You have travelled some distance,' he said.

Jolie, too, was stirred by the turn the conversation had taken. She had come to Cold Creek to find Sam Holland. Maybe this was the opening she had been looking for.

'I have come here hoping to meet with someone,' she said. 'An old acquaintance.'

'An old acquaintance?' There was a question in Taylor's voice, which she ignored.

'A friend of the family, you might say.'

'And you have reason to think he might be in Cold Creek?'

'I never said it was a man. In fact, you are right. His name is Sam Holland. I don't suppose you've come across him?'

Taylor's brows puckered as he thought for a few moments. 'No,' he concluded, 'I can't say that I have.'

'There's no reason why you should. It was a long shot.'

'I could make some inquiries,' he said.

'Thanks. I would appreciate that.'

Taylor's eyes swept the scene before

them before returning to his companion. 'Come on,' he said. 'Let's get back to the horses and ride on down to the bridge. I can tell you are a lady of taste. I'm sure that you will appreciate the inside of my house here at Valhalla.' They started to walk back along the path.

'It's an odd name for an estate,' Jolie said. 'Why do you call it Valhalla?'

'Valhalla, as you may know, is the final destination of warriors in Norse mythology. It is usually depicted as a magnificent, majestic hall situated in Asgard. Perhaps I am guilty of exaggeration, but I like to think of my home in that way.'

They quickly reached the horses and mounted. Looking about them as they rode, they started for the covered bridge.

★   ★   ★

Zip Short was furious with himself for having missed his chance to deal with

Wyeth. He knew he had wasted a golden opportunity. What was more, Wyeth had been warned. He knew now that someone was out to get him. He would take care to guard his back. Short had seen Wyeth ride into Cold Creek that first night with two others, so that meant he had friends. Things could get awkward. He needed to do something more drastic, and if it removed a possible threat posed by the other two, so much the better.

Returning to his dingy shack on the outskirts of town, Short made his way to the basement. There was a cupboard in one corner. He unlocked it and, carefully reaching inside, pulled out a large box from which he lifted a black, cast-iron ball with a long wooden tailpiece. A smile lifted the corners of his mouth as he weighed it in his hand. It felt good. It was a Ketchum hand grenade and he felt a kind of nostalgia flow over him as he held it. It seemed so long ago that he had thrown one. Maybe it was time to put that right.

There wouldn't be anything Wyeth could do once this little beauty was rigged and aimed in his direction. Then he thought again. No, something more was needed if he was to be quite sure of dealing with Wyeth and his two cronies. Gently, he replaced the grenade in the box and after a little fumbling in the cupboard, withdrew a couple of sticks of dynamite.

★   ★   ★

The day following his discussion with Shuman, Wyeth remained indoors. Rattlesnake was on the mend and it was with difficulty that he could be persuaded to remain in his bunk. Between them, Wyeth and Shuman tended to him, changing his dressings and keeping the wound clean. Although he knew from experience just how tough the oldster was, Wyeth was still surprised at his resilience. Eventually, he could be restrained no longer.

'No offence, Shuman, but I'm gettin'

kinda bored. I ain't used to this kinda high livin'.'

Shuman looked at him, suspecting irony, but Wyeth knew the oldster simply meant what he said. Rattlesnake was used to sleeping on the ground with his saddle for a pillow and the stars for a roof. For him, a bunk in a livery loft was luxury. The oldster had also spent time in detention at Andersonville. That had probably affected his scale of values.

'Why don't we all take a walk over to the Silver Dollar?' Rattlesnake said.

'I reckon you're forgettin' the reason you and Wyeth are holed up here,' Shuman replied.

'Ain't nobody gonna recognize us with these whiskers.'

'Wyeth has already proved that wrong,' Shuman said.

'You mean the bushwhackin'? That varmint's the low-down type who only shoots from cover. He might be skulkin' down some alley but he won't be facin' up in front of folks.'

'Hell, I'm beginnin' to get jumpy, too, hangin' about here all day,' Wyeth said. 'I reckon Rattlesnake's right.'

'I could do with a drink,' Shuman said.

Together, they stepped out into the evening. Lights were appearing up and down the main street. They walked side by side, Rattlesnake holding his arm stiffly by his side. They reached the Silver Dollar and, pushing through the batwing doors, entered the saloon. As soon as they reached the bar Wyeth sensed that something was wrong. The place was busy but the noise had quieted. Glancing in the mirror, he saw that a number of faces were turned in their direction.

'Whiskey,' he said. The bartender poured. 'Leave the bottle.'

Looking again into the mirror, he saw a man at one of the tables get to his feet and make his way to the batwings. As he left, he glanced back towards two other men, who had been sitting with him. As soon as the batwings closed behind him Wyeth knew he had gone to get the marshal.

'I think I've been recognized,' he said. 'Finish your drink and we'll get out of here.'

Rattlesnake and Shuman tossed back the whiskey. Then they turned and began to make their way towards the exit.

'You boys forgot the bottle,' the bartender called.

Wyeth didn't respond. His attention was on the two men at the table where the man who had left had been sitting. He was watching closely for any sudden movement when a voice rang out behind him.

'Stop right there!' The three of them did as the man commanded. At the same moment the two men Wyeth had been watching rose to their feet and drew their guns. The saloon was silent. All talk had stopped as the rest of the customers watched what was happening.

'What is this?' Wyeth said. He half turned.

'Stay still!' the voice rapped.

Wyeth had seen enough. The man barking out the orders was the bartender and he held a sawn-down shotgun, which he pointed at them. Wyeth glanced at Shuman. He knew exactly how Rattlesnake would react but Shuman was an unknown quantity.

'Take their guns,' the bartender snapped.

The two men took one step forward but before they had taken another Wyeth's gun was in his hand and spitting lead. Rattlesnake was an instant behind. The two men tumbled backwards and as the barman's shotgun boomed, Wyeth pushed Shuman. He fell sideways as buckshot tore around them. Wyeth spun round and fired. The barman staggered and then fell, dropping his weapon as he did so.

'Let's get out of here!' Wyeth shouted.

Shuman had recovered his balance and all three of them hurtled through the batwings. Down the street Wyeth could see the figure of the marshal together with another man, who Wyeth assumed was the man from the saloon. Behind them a third figure emerged, carrying a rifle. Wyeth guessed it was a deputy marshal. Scarcely pausing, Wyeth flung himself in the opposite direction, followed by Shuman and Rattlesnake. Voices began to call and then a shot rang out. Rattlesnake was finding it hard to run and glancing over his shoulder, Wyeth could see that the marshal was beginning to catch up with them.

'Aim for the alleyway!' he shouted. It seemed that he and that alleyway were destined for each other. Another glance behind, however, suggested that they would never make it. More people had appeared. The marshal and the deputy were closing fast and some of the shooting was getting uncomfortably close. Rattlesnake was clearly in difficulty. Things looked bad when suddenly there was a deafening roar and a sheet of flame rose into the air just behind them. Debris rained down as a cloud of smoke and dust obscured the marshal's party from view.

'That's the livery stables!' Shuman shouted.

'Keep going!' Wyeth replied.

He saw their one chance of escape in the confusion and uproar caused by the explosion. They clattered down the alley and, reaching the end, turned along a side street. A short distance brought them to a junction and they turned down another narrow street. Wyeth was growing more confident with every stride. The alleyway was the one his would-be assassin had chosen, and he knew he would have chosen it for a reason; it provided a good getaway. After continuing a little way they drew to a halt.

'I'm about done in,' Rattlesnake gasped.

Wyeth turned to Shuman. 'What's the best way now?' he said. Behind them they could hear the sounds of pursuit being taken up again.

'Follow me!' Shuman said.

They started forwards once more and in a few moments took another turn. Wyeth was getting confused. He wasn't sure in which direction they were now heading. By the same token, he figured, their pursuers would be even more confused. They carried on running till they crossed an open space. Looking to his right, Wyeth could see some lights, which he guessed were those of the town. A cloud of smoke hung in the air. They had slowed now but presently, finding that they were in some woods, they felt relatively safe. It was only when they had gone a little further and began to breathe in the acrid smell of burning that Wyeth realized they were approaching the back of the livery stables. The flickering and crackling of fire became evident.

'Hell, shouldn't we be goin' a different way?' Wyeth asked. 'We're right back in town.'

'Yeah, but that's just where they won't be expectin' us to be. Besides, we set off in one direction and we've come back from another. But more important than all that, we need to get our horses.'

Wyeth grinned. 'Shuman,' he said, 'I got to hand it to you.'

They came through the trees and had their first glimpse of the damage that had been wrought to the livery stables. The whole building was virtually a ruin. One side had been blown out and the other walls sagged. The roof had collapsed.

'Hell, it's lucky we put our mounts in the outside corral,' Rattlesnake said.

The horses were frightened and it took some moments to quieten them. Their saddles were hanging on the fence rails and the men quickly fastened them. There were things Wyeth wanted to say, but they all knew they could not delay; it was only a matter of time till the marshal would arrive. Once he realized that they had got away, it wouldn't take long for him to raise a posse. They needed to get going and put as much ground as possible between them and the town. For a moment Shuman stood and regarded the devastation to his livery stables before they all swung into leather and began to ride away through the trees.

They rode through the rest of the night, pacing the horses, and only as the first light of pre-dawn began to gleam did they come to a halt. Rattlesnake's wound had opened up and begun to bleed and Shuman tended to it while Wyeth built up a fire. Their meal was limited to cold strips of jerky but they had coffee in their saddle-bags and tobacco. When they had eaten and made themselves as comfortable as circumstances would allow, Wyeth turned awkwardly to Shuman.

'I don't know what to say,' he began.

'You don't need to say anythin'.'

'We did wrong to involve you in all this. Now, because of us, you ain't got a place to go back to.'

'What the hell happened back there?' Rattlesnake interposed.

Wyeth turned to him. 'Someone targeted the livery stables. He must have seen us go in and out. I figure it must be the varmint who tried to shoot me, but I don't know why he would have targeted you and Shuman as well.'

'One thing's for sure,' Rattlesnake replied. 'Whoever he is, he ain't just a bounty hunter.'

'It's not only Wyeth he has to answer to now,' Shuman said. 'I aim to get even with that bastard.'

'I'm sorry for what's happened,' Wyeth said. 'Me and Rattlesnake both.'

'Well I ain't,' Shuman said. 'Look, neither of you has anythin' to apologize for. I knowed what I was doin' right from the start.' He suddenly laughed. 'Well, maybe I didn't reckon with the livery stables bein' blown to kingdom come. I guess we should be countin' our lucky stars. It was just plumb good fortune we weren't inside when it blew.'

'What do you reckon it was?' Rattlesnake said. 'Dynamite?'

'Yeah. I figured maybe a grenade, but

a grenade wouldn't have had so big an effect. The war's over, but there's a whole lot of that kinda stuff still in peoples' hands.'

'What's that you say?' Shuman said. 'The war's over? I figured you folks were all for carryin' it on.' Wyeth didn't respond. He realized himself the significance of his words. There was a moment's silence broken only by the crackling of the fire. 'I hope you ain't changed your minds just when I've joined the cause,' Shuman joked.

Wyeth took a drink of coffee. He drew cigarette smoke into his lungs and then blew it out in rings. Rattlesnake observed him. 'Is somethin' botherin' you?' he said.

Wyeth took a moment to reply. 'I was just thinkin' about those three we shot,' he replied.

'They didn't give us any option,' Rattlesnake said. 'Either we fought our way out of there or we ended up on a gallows. If we managed to escape a lynchin', that is.'

'I don't know,' Wyeth said, and then added somewhat inconsequentially, 'maybe they weren't hurt too bad. Maybe they'll pull through.'

'They ain't got a doc now,' Rattlesnake commented. 'We got him.'

Wyeth turned to Shuman. 'You haven't got a choice now,' he said. 'You're an outlaw, just like us.'

Shuman grinned. 'In that case,' he said, 'when do we pull that bank job?'

'After what's happened, I reckon we just about cooked our goose so far as Cold Creek is concerned,' Wyeth said.

'As far as I can see, that only gives us all the more reason to hit back,' Shuman replied.

'That's the way I see it, too,' Rattlesnake said.

'You old goat, you ain't fit yet,' Wyeth retorted.

'Like I been tellin' you, I'm fine now. This here is child's play compared with the war.'

'Time's passed. You were younger then. We all were.'

'If I didn't know you, I'd say you were gettin' soft.'

'I'm gettin' tired,' Wyeth responded. 'I figure we could all do with snatchin' some sleep.'

Shuman was thoughtful. 'Have you two considered this?' he said. 'If the marshal comes after us with a posse, the town's gonna be wide open. It could be just the right time to carry out a robbery.'

Rattlesnake chuckled. 'Yeah,' he said. 'You got a good point there. Now we're on the run, nobody would be expectin' us to ride right back again.'

'And don't forget,' Shuman added. 'We all got a score to settle with that varmint who blew up the livery stables. Whoever he is.'

Wyeth turned to him. 'That reminds me,' he said. 'I still got a date with Kirby Taylor at that place of his. What was it called?'

'The Valhalla,' Shuman replied.

* * *

The interior of Taylor's house was just as impressive as the exterior. The main hall was spacious, with a large chandelier and a wide, semi-circular stairway leading to the floor above. Pictures hung on the wall. Taylor paused just long enough for Jolie to admire it before leading the way to a door on the right. It opened into a parlour filled with sunlight, which streamed in through deep-set windows and fell on the richly carpeted floor. There were a number of horsehair chairs and sofas with antimacassars and, in a corner near the window overlooking a lawn, a solid mahogany desk. Taylor led the way to the window and invited Jolie to view the prospect. The room was at the side of the house and the lawn was a continuation of the one she had seen at the front. It led down to a narrow creek lined with cedar and willow.

'It is a beautiful scene,' Jolie said. 'To some extent it reminds me of some of the views on my father's ranch.'

'You were born there? Forgive my memory; what did you say it was called?'

'The Barbed R. Not a very romantic name I'm afraid. Yes, I was born there, born and raised. Although I've only been away such a short time, I'm missing it already.'

Taylor had been thinking about what Jolie had said previously. As soon as she mentioned the name of the ranch again he made the connection. The Barbed R was the name of the place Zip Short had mentioned.

'Hopefully, you won't need to be away from it for too long,' he said. 'With any luck, we should be able to locate the gentleman you came to see. What was his name?'

'Sam Holland.'

'Ah yes. A family friend, you said. I don't think you mentioned what business he had in Cold Creek.'

'I'm not sure myself. He only mentioned the name in passing.'

'What does he look like? To have a

description might help trace him.'

'Oh, I don't know. Nothing special, I guess.'

Taylor had a sudden inspiration. In a desk in his study he had a copy of the Wanted poster on Eugene Wyeth. It was a long shot, but if he cut out the picture and showed it to her, what would her reaction be?

'I have an idea,' he said. 'If you would excuse me for a moment, I'll be right back.'

He turned and left the room. Jolie was slightly surprised at his departure but she didn't have much time to think about it before he was back holding a piece of paper in his hand.

'I wonder if you might take a look at this,' he said.

He held the paper out. There was a puzzled look on Jolie's face as she took it. When she saw the picture, a gasp of surprise escaped her.

'Where did you get this?' she said.

'You recognize the man?'

'Yes, of course. It's Sam, Sam

Holland. The man I have come to meet. But I don't understand. What are you doing with a picture of him?' She looked at Taylor and suddenly she was frightened. His expression had changed and there was anger in his eyes.

'That man,' he said, 'is a wanted renegade. His name is not Sam Holland but Eugene Wyeth. Worst of all, he is a traitor to the Confederacy.'

'The Confederacy?' she murmured, not comprehending.

'I'm afraid I shall have to detain you here,' Taylor said. 'If there's a chance that this man is in the vicinity, for the sake of lawful folk I can't let you go.'

'What do you mean? You can't keep me here.'

'I have every reason to do so. Quite apart from any other consideration, from what you have told me I have reason to deduce that you are complicit with a wanted outlaw.'

'I don't understand. You can't mean what you're saying.' By way of answer

146

Taylor rang a bell, which stood on the mantelpiece. In a few seconds a man appeared.

'Pritchard, take this young lady and put her in the library. Make sure she does not leave.'

The man grinned. 'Sure, boss,' he said. He seized Jolie by the arm and she began to struggle.

'I would advise you not to resist,' Taylor said. 'I'm afraid Mr Pritchard has his own ways of being persuasive.'

Jolie felt the man's grip tighten on her arm. 'He's hurting me!' she shouted.

'As I say, Mr Pritchard has his own methods. I can't say that I agree with them, but I suggest you allow him to escort you to the library.'

The man began to drag her away and her resistance flagged. Taylor watched as Pritchard disappeared with the girl through the door. Then he sat down at the mahogany desk to consider how best to make capital of his unexpected windfall. Not having made use of the services of Miss Hoskins just recently, the fortuitous arrival of Jolie Rawley might serve his purposes in more ways than one.

7

Wyeth, Rattlesnake and Shuman rode slowly, taking their time about getting back to Cold Creek. They were fairly certain that a posse would be on their trail, and they kept on the alert for any signs of it. Wyeth and Rattlesnake were enjoying themselves. This was just like it used to be during the war years. They had no fear of being caught. For men who had fought with Jeb Stuart and operated behind enemy lines, it was child's play.

'Remember how we rode clear round McLellan?' Rattlesnake said.

'I remember the Bower,' Wyeth replied.

Rattlesnake laughed as he, too, recalled the days when they were in camp in the valley of the Blue Ridge Mountains. Life there was one huge party at the big rambling house before they received their orders to raid into Maryland. They had ridden 130 miles in three days on that occasion, circling the entire Union Army of the Potomac with minimal losses and sixty horses abandoned, worn out from the hectic pace. Yes, this was truly child's play.

They heard the posse before they had a sight of it and had plenty of time to conceal themselves. There were half a dozen riders and they were moving very slowly.

'I figure they could do with a tracker,' Shuman commented.

'At least they're travellin' the right way,' Wyeth said. 'Wonder how long they'll keep on goin'?'

They had left Cold Creek in a hurry and it was relatively easy for the posse to follow their trail. But now they had taken care to cover their tracks. As Wyeth had done previously, they were taking a roundabout route, and it was unlikely that the marshal would be able to pick up their sign.

When the posse had passed by they

rode out of cover and carried on towards Cold Creek. Wyeth had already briefed them about the layout of the bank. He would have liked to plan the operation in more detail, but circumstances decreed otherwise. He agreed with Shuman. If they were going to hit the bank, the time to do it was when the marshal was out of town with the posse. What they lacked in preparation they would make up for with the element of surprise.

★   ★   ★

Jolie Rawley was taken totally aback by the situation in which she now found herself, but when she started to think about it, she realized how naïve she had been. She had been taken in by Kirby Taylor's surface charm and had only herself to blame for the way things had turned out. She should have known better than to compromise herself in any way. Her only excuse was that she had had an ulterior motive in accepting

Taylor's attention; he seemed to be the ideal person to help her find Sam Holland. In a way, she had been proved right. As it turned out, Taylor did know about Holland. She thought about his words. What did he mean when he said that Holland was a traitor to the Confederacy? She knew something of Sam Holland's activities. She would have had to be even more naïve than she had proved not to have done so. She had chosen not to push things, not to look too closely at what Sam might be involved in. But one thing she did know: whatever he had done, it was because of his allegiance to the Confederacy. It all seemed somewhat strange to her. The days of the Confederacy and of the war were over. Wasn't it time everyone accepted that fact?

★   ★   ★

Zip Short was in something of a quandary. He had carried out his attack on the livery stables. Coming on it from the concealment of the woods, he had dynamited the place. Nobody could have escaped the blast. Then, just when he should have been enjoying the fruits of his endeavours, it seemed that Wyeth and his cronies might have survived after all. He had emerged from cover to find that a considerable amount of activity was taking place in town, but had assumed it was in the aftermath of the blast. He hadn't been too concerned. But then the rumours began to fly and the next thing he knew was that the marshal was organizing a posse to go after three men who had caused a disturbance in the Silver Dollar saloon. One of the men had been recognized as Eugene Wyeth, the man whose Wanted poster adorned several walls around town.

For a while he considered joining the posse but finally he rejected the idea. What would be the point? Knowing something about Wyeth and his methods, he doubted that the marshal would catch up with him. If he did, and Wyeth was either killed or arrested, it wouldn't do Short any favours. Wyeth would have escaped the vengeance of the black skull. Working on the hypothesis that the posse would have no success, Short decided that the best thing would be to stay his hand and wait to see what happened. In the meantime, he needed to report back to Kirby Taylor on developments. Taylor had stressed that he wanted to be kept informed and Short had no desire to go against his orders or upset him. He knew better.

★   ★   ★

Once they were within sight of town, Wyeth drew his two companions to a halt.

'Everyone know what to do? Rattlesnake, you wait outside with the horses; I'll make the approach to the teller. Shuman, you keep an eye on the inner office. Just take it easy. We don't want anybody gettin' hurt.'

'It ain't nothin' we haven't done before,' Rattlesnake said.

'You're quite sure you're OK carryin' that wound?'

'Shuman's done a great job. Hell, I'm feelin' better than I did before I got shot.'

'Like I just said, we want to avoid any lead being flung. It doesn't matter if we don't get all the loot as long as we get enough that they'll remember us by. When we hightail it out of town, remember we head for the Valhalla. Shuman, you take the lead and show us the way.'

'You really figure that Kirby Taylor's involved in tryin' to kill you?' Shuman said.

'Yeah. I've been thinkin' about it. And it's not just me he's tried to kill. We're all lucky to be alive after what happened to Shuman's livery stables.'

'Not to mention the Silver Dollar incident,' Rattlesnake grinned.

'Things have certainly livened up since I met you boys,' Shuman said.

'I'm kinda wonderin' what you got up your sleeves for when we finish here.'

'We'll think of somethin',' Rattle-snake replied.

'We got plenty on our hands right now,' Wyeth said, 'without concernin' ourselves about the future. Let's get on with it.'

*　　*　　*

Jolie Rawley wasn't the sort of girl to spend all her time thinking and worrying. If she was, she would never have ventured on the journey to Cold Creek. Once her initial shock was over, she began to look round for a way to escape. The obvious places to check were the windows and the doors, but as she expected they were all fastened. She knew that the man who had been assigned to keep guard was just outside. Taylor had described the room as a library. That might have been its original purpose but there was only one bookshelf over which hung a lurid picture of some mythological scene. It seemed to function more as a study. There was a drinks cabinet but the main feature of the room was a big stone-built hearth. Jolie recalled the outward appearance of the house and the prominence of the single chimney. It seemed that it must be a central feature of the building. It was a fair guess that the chimney ran from the cellar to the roof.

Moving to the hearth, she peered up the flue. It was brick-built and the bricks were large and uneven. There was a slight ledge and the chimney itself was surprisingly clean. She guessed that it had something to do with its construction. Above her, the gloom was relieved by patches of light. Her heart began to beat harder. Could the chimney offer a possible way out? The patches of light were probably the hearth on the next floor and, high above, a narrow patch of sky. She wouldn't have far to climb to the next storey. It was when she looked down, however, that her courage failed. As she had supposed, the chimney began in the cellar. Below her was what seemed to be a dark abyss. It was in vain that she tried to comfort herself with the thought that even if she slipped, she would not have far to fall. It was of little use to try and think logically. She had no way of measuring the actual distance and the plunge appeared dreadful.

She looked up again. The brickwork was very uneven and offered plenty of hand and foot holds. If it wasn't for the drop, she would have felt confident of being able to climb to the next floor. It was fortunate that she was wearing a riding outfit. Taking a deep breath, she put her foot on the ledge and stood inside the chimney. The ledge was narrow. There was scarcely room for both her feet. She looked around for the next projection. The chimney was just narrow enough for her to be able to straddle it. She saw a gap in the brickwork a little above and on the opposite side and put her foot in it.

Clutching at the chimney wall, she swung out over the void.

She had committed herself now. There was nothing she could do but hold on and look for the next foothold. She concentrated on looking upwards, making a conscious effort not to glance down. The chimney itself seemed to moan with a faint soughing of the captured wind. Slowly, she heaved herself up, taking time to rest and recover her breath each time she clung to a new hold. Soon her arms began to ache and her hands were cut and scraped from the roughness of the bricks. When she was about half way to the next storey she thought she heard voices. She listened attentively but the sound faded away. Maybe it was someone talking inside the house or maybe it was just an effect of the peculiar acoustics of the chimney. Suddenly her foot slipped and for a moment she thought she was going to fall, but she managed to hold on. She pressed herself against the wall of the chimney, clinging on with all her might. She felt her legs begin to shake and realized that she was sobbing. She needed to move on before her nerve gave way.

Despairingly, she sought a projection or a gap that would be large enough to bear her weight. It was lucky that she was light. A vision crossed her mind, a memory of how she would climb the apple trees in her father's orchard behind the ranch when she was young. She had often climbed there. Maybe that experience was standing her in good stead. Putting the recollection from her mind, she chose her next holds and trusted herself to the chimney wall. As she climbed the chimney grew lighter and she realized she must be close to her target. She looked up and saw the gap that indicated the hearth she was trying to reach. Now a new fear struck her. What if the room she was approaching was occupied? There was nothing she could do about it. There was no way she could go any further. Trying to make as little sound as possible, she came level to the opening and struggled to get her body across it. Her arms were through and she made a final heave. Her muscles seemed to crack as she hauled herself over the ledge and slithered, exhausted, through the grate.

She lay still for a few moments before sitting up to take stock of her surroundings. She was in a room furnished in a similar way to the first room she had been in. Getting to her feet, she tiptoed to the door. She carefully turned the handle and the door opened on to a passageway at the end of which was the semi-circular staircase. Scarcely daring to breathe, she crept down the passage and descended the stairs. When she reached the hall she stopped. It was deserted. She could see the door to the parlour where Taylor had first led her. Was he still in there? Unfortunately, the door was partly open. Should she try to find some other way out? After a few moments thought she decided to risk crossing the hall.

Taking off her shoes and holding them carefully, she was about to start when the door to the parlour was flung wide open and Taylor came out. Making herself as small and inconspicuous as possible, she shrank back against the wall. Taylor passed close by, his face intent, oblivious to his surroundings. She could scarcely breathe due to fear and tension, and now she had another thing to worry about: Was he on his way to the library? If so, he would quickly find that she was gone. She had to take a calculated risk. Getting to her feet she began to run across the hallway, praying that the door would not be locked. Breathlessly, she fumbled at the door handle and, to her relief, it opened. She slipped through it, quietly closed it behind her, and put her shoes back on. What was she to do now? She took a look around. The stable buildings were at the back of the house. Should she make her way round the side of the building and try to find her horse? The prospect before her was open. In all likelihood, she would be spotted as soon as she appeared. She remembered the sight she had seen of the side of the house. There was an open stretch there, too, but it wasn't anywhere near so long. It led down to a stream and the shelter of trees. She came to a decision and moved to the corner of the building. Then she began to sprint as hard as she could.

★ ★ ★

Leaving their horses in the care of Rattlesnake, Wyeth and Shuman stepped up onto the boardwalk and entered the bank. It was quiet inside. Wyeth had deliberately timed their arrival for shortly after noon when a lot of people would be indoors having lunch and the bank staffing likely to be depleted. The same cashier that Wyeth had observed on his previous visit was on duty. With the merest nod to Shuman to indicate that he was going ahead, Wyeth approached the man. He was taking a chance that he might recognize him from his Wanted poster but he was not concerned otherwise about concealing his identity. It was too late to worry about that. As the cashier looked up, Wyeth produced a fifty dollar bill from his pocket.

'I wonder if you could change this?' he said.

The cashier took it and held it up to the light. Something about it seemed to trouble him and he looked at it more intently. When he eventually looked back at Wyeth, he found himself staring into the muzzle of .44.

'Don't make any silly moves,' Wyeth said. 'Just do as I say and nobody gets hurt.' The man nodded. Wyeth handed him a cloth bag. 'Go to the safe, open it and fill the bag,' he said.

'The safe is in the manager's office,' the cashier replied.

'Yeah. That's why my friend will accompany you.'

The cashier looked up and seemed to notice Shuman for the first time as he stepped forward. A flicker of recognition passed across his features but quickly vanished as he got up from his chair to accompany the oldster to the back office. The door opened and then closed behind them. Only one other person had entered the bank and appeared not to have noticed that anything out of the ordinary was taking place. He stood near to Wyeth, waiting for the cashier to return. A shaft of sunlight entered the room from a window high up in the wall and Wyeth observed the motes illuminated by it. The gun was now concealed inside his jacket and he was feeling icy cool, even when the door opened and a tall man wearing the star of a deputy marshal walked in.

Wyeth glanced towards the door of the inner office. Shuman should be emerging any moment with the cashier and the bag of money; maybe with the bank manager, too, if he was in there. There was little chance that the deputy marshal would not recognize Wyeth from the Wanted poster. Wyeth remained unperturbed, keenly aware of the situation, but trying to think logically, when there was a sudden eruption of noise from outside. The deputy marshal and the man standing near Wyeth both turned their heads towards the door and the next moment it flew open and a man, who was obviously drunk, staggered into the room. For a moment Wyeth was confused till he recognized Rattle-snake.

'Where's the marshal?' Rattlesnake shouted. He stared round the room till his eyes alighted on the deputy. 'Marshal,' he mouthed, 'what are you going to do about it?'

The deputy stepped forward and took him by the arm. 'Do about what?' he said. 'What are you talkin' about?'

'I'm talkin' about those low-down

stinkin' galoots outside who took my wallet.'

'You're drunk,' the deputy marshal said.

Rattlesnake began to struggle and the deputy pushed him towards the exit. Just as they passed outside, the inner door to the manager's office opened and the cashier appeared carrying the bag; Shuman followed closely behind. There was no sign of the manager. Shuman moved towards the door while the cashier took his seat once more behind the counter. His eyes flickered for a moment past Wyeth towards the man still standing behind him.

'Hand the bag over,' Wyeth said quietly. The cashier did so. 'And don't think about any heroics. My partner's gun will be pointed right in your direction. Just carry on as normal. Serve the next customer. You understand?'

The cashier nodded. Wyeth turned away and began to walk towards the door where Shuman had halted. As

Wyeth walked past he gave Shuman a nod and the ostler followed him through the door and into the street. For a moment Wyeth's eyes were dazzled by the sunlight but they quickly adjusted as he looked round, searching for the horses. In a few seconds he located them. Rattlesnake had tied them to a hitch-rack just across the street. But where was Rattlesnake? There was no time to waste. Wyeth and Shuman strode rapidly across the street, untied the horses and mounted. They swung away, Wyeth leading Rattlesnake's mount by the reins.

'What about Rattlesnake?' Shuman hissed.

Before Wyeth could reply, there was a loud shout and the door of the bank flew open. The cashier, recognizing them, lifted a rifle.

'Ride!' Wyeth shouted.

The cashier opened fire just as Wyeth and Shuman dug in their spurs. Wyeth heard the singing of lead as it flew past his head but the man's aim was erratic.

Shuman had drawn his pistol and was about to return fire when Wyeth called to him. 'Leave it! We're nearly out of range!'

As if to deny his assertion, he felt a tug at his jacket as the next bullet flew uncomfortably close. They both ducked low. Wyeth glanced back. To his astonishment a figure burst out of a group of bystanders who had gathered at the commotion and, running hard, crashed into the cashier, whose rifle was still raised to his shoulder. The man ran on and Wyeth suddenly realized it was Rattlesnake. Leaving Shuman to continue, he slowed his horse as the oldster continued running. The cashier had been taken out of action but someone else had commenced shooting and Wyeth saw that it was the deputy marshal. Rattlesnake was slowing and Wyeth backed the horses. Blowing hard, the oldster came up alongside his horse. He put his foot in the stirrup and swung aboard. In a matter of seconds the horses were running and picking up speed. Some further bullets sang through the air but they were quickly out of range. Shuman had slowed and they caught him up.

'Keep goin'!' Wyeth shouted. 'Let's lose 'em.'

Digging in their spurs, they rode hard out of town. Shuman knew the country well and soon he had led them off the main trail. He took them through a stand of trees, following a game trail that eventually led to a shallow wash. They splashed their way through it to emerge into a stretch of rough, broken country. The horses were beginning to suffer and they slowed to a walking pace.

'Nobody's gonna find us,' Shuman said. 'We've got nothin' to worry about.'

'That was a mighty close run thing,' Wyeth said. 'If it wasn't for Rattle-snake's quick thinkin', I figure we'd have had our chips.'

'I was holdin' on to the horses like we arranged when I saw the deputy comin' down the street,' Rattlesnake replied. 'I figured to come in to the bank to warn you boys but by the time I got those horses tied to the hitch-rail, he had already gone inside. I reckoned the only thing to do was to create some kind of disturbance.'

'Your actin' had me convinced,' Wyeth said.

'Put it down to the time I worked for a travellin' show,' Rattlesnake replied.

Wyeth turned to Shuman. 'You didn't have any trouble with the manager?' he said.

'He wasn't there. Guess we just struck it lucky.' Shuman eyed the bag, which was laid across Wyeth's saddle. 'Why don't we take a peek?' he said. 'See how much we've taken.'

They came to a halt and Wyeth slung the bag to Shuman, who dug inside. His hand emerged holding a wad of bills. He began to count. When he had finished he drew out another wad and continued doing so till he had accounted for it all.

'Near enough sixteen thousand dollars in notes and a heap of gold coins beside.' Rattlesnake whooped and they all began to laugh.

'Sixteen thousand less fifty dollars,' Wyeth said. The others looked at him. 'That's what I gave the cashier,' he added. 'I plumb forgot to get it back.'

They burst into laughter again. Eventually Wyeth took a look around.

'How far to the Valhalla?' he said.

'I haven't forgot,' Shuman replied. 'We might have taken a roundabout route, but we're headed that way.'

Wyeth nodded. 'Good,' he said. 'Our business ain't but half completed. Once the horses have had a break, I figure it's time we paid a visit to Mr Kirby Taylor.'

★ ★ ★

Jolie Rawley ran as hard as she could down the grassy slope leading to the stream. When she reached it she flung herself down the bank and into the water where she took a tumble.

Fortunately the water was shallow but when she stood up she was thoroughly wet. She began to move down the stream, feeling a little more secure now she was screened, to some extent, from the house. Her one idea was to get as far away as possible and she kept on moving. She was unsure of her bearings but followed the drift of the stream, assuming it would lead her to the river. From there she would try to reach the covered bridge. After all her exertions she felt weary and wondered whether it might not after all have been a better idea to try and find her horse. But she would have made herself too conspicuous that way.

She struggled on, occasionally pausing to look around her and listen for any sounds of pursuit. The stream took a wide curve and, unexpectedly, she saw where it debouched into the river ahead. It seemed fair to assume that the river, too, was shallow, but she didn't want to take any unnecessary risk and she climbed back up the bank. It was darker among the trees and for the first time she felt a shiver of apprehension. So far, she had been too occupied with making her escape to think about anything else, but she suddenly realized the gravity of her situation. Quite apart from the threat posed by Taylor, she would have to face the prospect of a night alone, a long way from anywhere. Trying to steady her nerves and concentrate on the matter in hand, she continued to move. The rippling of the waters was louder now. When she looked through the intervening trees, she saw that the river was wider and flowing more quickly. She peered ahead, trying to see the covered bridge. She couldn't be certain that she had turned the right way, or if she had, whether it was the best idea to make for the bridge. She had a vague idea that at least that way she might hope to meet with someone. She didn't consider the fact that she was on private property and anyone she would be likely to meet would be in Taylor's employ. She staggered and stumbled on, following the course of the river, until eventually she saw what she had been looking for; the covered bridge. The sight of it gave her fresh courage and she began to run. She had almost reached it when she heard a sound which made her blood run cold. It was the sound of voices. Her escape had been discovered. Taylor and his men were not far behind.

★　★　★

After Jolie Rawley had been taken to the library, Kirby Taylor sat down and looked hard at the Wanted poster picture of Eugene Wyeth. If the girl had made all the effort to follow him to Cold Creek, it was almost certain he was somewhere in the vicinity. It was also fairly certain that there was some sort of relationship between them. A scheme began to hatch itself in his brain. If Wyeth could be informed that Jolie Rawley was being held at the Valhalla, he wouldn't waste any time in following her there. An ugly leer began to spread across his countenance. It would be an easy enough matter to spread the word, just as he had spread the word about the fake payroll. Who knew? It might not be necessary to do even that. Wyeth seemed to have his own ways and means of gathering information and acting on it. Maybe he was on his way to the Valhalla at that very moment. Either way, it would be as well to be prepared. He rang the bell once more and another of his lackeys appeared.

'Tell the boys to get ready,' he said.

'All of 'em?'

'Yeah. All of 'em.'

The man didn't need any further encouragement. Turning on his heel, he made his way out of the room. It was good that something seemed to be happening. For too long Taylor's bunch of desperados had been kicking their heels. They needed some action. Without something to occupy them, they tended to get restless. Taylor's evil grin became wider as he realized how restless he was feeling since spending time with Jolie Rawley. She was quite a woman. Why wait any longer to enjoy her? He got to his feet and left the room. A short walk brought him to the library where the man he had assigned to guard Jolie sat on a chair outside the door.

'I take it there have been no difficulties with the lady?' Taylor said.

'No, sir. She's been quiet as a snake with no rattles.'

Taylor leered. 'Time we changed that, I think.'

Pritchard grinned back. He was used to his boss's ways. Taylor opened the door to the library and went inside. He could not immediately see the woman. He looked around the room. No sign of her. He walked to the window and looked behind the curtains. He checked that the windows were bolted. Then he looked round the room again, his brows lowering.

'Pritchard!' he called.

The door opened and the guard entered. 'What is it, Mr Taylor?' he said.

Taylor's face was twisted in rage. 'Take a look around,' he replied.

The man did so and then turned to Taylor with a puzzled expression. 'I don't get it,' he said. 'Where is the lady?'

'I thought you might be able to answer that question,' Taylor snapped.

'She's got to be here,' Pritchard began, but he didn't get any further. Before he could continue Taylor's gun had spoken and he staggered back with a bullet in his chest. Taylor fired again and Pritchard went down, twitching on the carpet. Taylor's finger squeezed the trigger once more and the man lay still. Without bothering to inspect his handiwork, Taylor stormed from the room and made his way to the hallway. He flung open the outer door and with no break in his stride rounded the corner of the house. A couple of his men appeared.

'Everything OK, Mr Taylor? We

thought we heard shots.'

'One of you go into the house and search for a woman. The other round up the boys and follow me.'

The men looked puzzled but didn't argue. Taylor stormed on. He didn't imagine Jolie would be found in the house. He didn't know how, but he was certain that she had got away. She hadn't been gone long, however, and there was nowhere for her to hide. He was certain to find her, and when he did he would teach her a lesson she would never forget.

8

Zip Short was approaching the covered bridge on his way to Valhalla when he saw a bedraggled figure approaching him across it from the other side. He slowed his horse to a walking pace and drew his gun. The figure was that of a young woman and she was waving her arms at him. He rode alongside her and came to a halt.

'Help me!' she exclaimed.

He got down from his horse and holstered his gun, then stood hesitating, not knowing what to make of the apparition.

'Help me!' she repeated before suddenly flinging herself upon him. He held his arms out, unsure whether to put them about her or not. His horse sidestepped and flung up its head, its nostrils quivering. He looked towards it.

'Whoa boy!' he said. Something was upsetting it. He was getting more confused by the moment. Coming from one direction he heard the sound of voices and then, from another, he thought he heard the faint sound of hoof beats. What was going on? At that moment a couple of figures appeared at the far end of the bridge, rapidly followed by some more. A voice called out loudly.

'Grab the woman! Don't let her get away!'

He looked down at Jolie at the same moment as she looked at him. For an instant their eyes met. Then he shrank back in pain as her nails clawed his face. She pushed hard and he staggered back. Before he had time to react, she had seized the reins of his horse and swung herself into the saddle. He made a grab for the horse and it reared into the air. He lost his balance and almost fell under its hoofs before Jolie got control and started to ride away.

'Stop her!' a voice yelled, but it was

too late. As the first of Taylor's men ran up, she had reached the opposite end of the bridge. Short whipped out his gun and was about to fire when somebody knocked it from his hand.

'Don't be stupid!' the man hissed. 'Taylor wants her alive.'

Short looked at him in puzzlement. The man drew his own gun and, taking careful aim, fired at the rapidly retreating horse. The horse ran on and the man fired again. This time it swerved before sinking to its knees. Jolie screamed and rolled clear as it fell over on its side. She had sufficient presence of mind to get to her feet and begin running.

'Quick! Go get her!' the man ordered.

Short was staring open-mouthed. His face hurt and blood was running down his cheek into his mouth. He was even more stupefied when the figure of Taylor appeared. 'I know this man,' he said, and turning to Short: 'I'll talk to you later.'

Jolie was running frantically. The horse had not gone very far before being brought down and she struggled to try and keep ahead of her pursuers. She was already exhausted, however, and she realized with despair that there was no way she could get away. They were closing in on her rapidly and she had all but given up hope when she suddenly became aware that a group of riders had appeared a little way ahead. They were riding fast towards her and her first thought was that they must be some more of Taylor's men. She veered away and flung herself into the undergrowth as a shot rang out. She raised her head as the riders came abreast of her and one of them jumped from his horse. He came running towards her and she shrank back, expecting the worst. The man was beside her and she raised an arm to protect herself, anticipating a blow. The blow did not come. Instead she found that she was being taken into the man's arms but it was only when she heard her name being spoken and she looked into his face that she realized it was Sam Holland: the man Taylor had referred to as Eugene Wyeth.

'Jolie,' he breathed. She put her arms around his neck and began to sob uncontrollably. Taking her in his arms, he carried her to a nearby stand of trees and placed her carefully on the ground. Behind them a fresh burst of gunfire resounded.

'I got to get back,' he said, 'but don't worry. Wait here. Don't move. I won't be long.' He began to take off his jacket in order to lay it over her but she suddenly sat up.

'What are you doing?' he said.

'What do you think?' she replied. 'I'm coming with you.' Shots were ringing out from the direction of the covered bridge.

'It's too dangerous,' Wyeth said.

'I'll take my chances,' she replied. 'I've come too far to let you go now.'

He looked at her and then took her in his arms again. 'I don't know how you got here,' he said. 'Explanations will have to wait. But I don't intend letting you go either.' For a few moments more he held her till she gently pushed him aside.

'I'm fine now,' she said. 'Come on, we can't stay here.'

Wyeth's every instinct was to remain with Jolie and protect her but he knew that the others were in a fight and that there was no way he could make her stay. There was a part of him, too, that had no desire to try. Together, they stood up and began to make their way towards the shooting. Wyeth was trying to work out what could have happened to Rattlesnake and Shuman. Looking towards the covered bridge, he caught a glimpse of men moving about. He drew his six-guns but he needed his rifle. He looked about him and was relieved to see his horse standing not far away. He whistled and the horse began to walk towards them.

'Good boy,' he whispered, when he had taken it by the reins. He led the steeldust into shelter and tied it to a tree before reaching forwards to draw his rifle from its scabbard. As he moved away Jolie put a hand on his arm.

'What about me?' she said. He didn't understand what she meant.

'I know how to use a gun, too,' she explained. For a moment he hesitated, reluctant to allow her to take any risks, but then he handed her one of his six-guns. Without further discussion, they began to make their way towards the bridge. He still had no idea what had happened to Rattlesnake and Shuman. Shots reverberated from the direction of the bridge but the tempo seemed to have quietened. He was trying to decide what best to do when he heard his name being called.

'Wyeth! Are you OK?' It was Rattlesnake.

'Yeah!' he called back. 'Where are you?'

'Over here! Both of us.'

Wyeth looked in the direction of the sound and saw something move in a patch of bushes. An arm appeared, waving. Wyeth expected Rattlesnake's voice to draw a fresh fusillade of shots but there wasn't any response from the direction of the bridge. Rattlesnake and Shuman had chosen a good spot. Putting Jolie behind him, Wyeth began to inch his way towards them. There was plenty of brush to help conceal them except for one stretch of more open ground towards the end.

'Give us cover!' Wyeth shouted.

As Rattlesnake and Shuman opened fire on the bridge, he and Jolie sprang forward and threw themselves into the shelter of the bushes. In a moment they had recovered their breath. Wyeth looked at Rattlesnake and Shuman.

'I'd like you to meet Miss Jolie Rawley,' he said.

Rattlesnake's face suddenly broke into a grin. 'Pleased to meet you,' he said to Jolie. He turned to Wyeth. 'Isn't she the gal — '

'Yes,' Wyeth interrupted. 'But don't ask me what she's doin' here.'

Shuman and Jolie shook hands. Rattlesnake was about to speak again but Wyeth beat him to it.

'Look,' he said, 'there's a whole lot of explainin' to be done, but it'll have to wait. Right now we got these varmints to deal with. Who do you reckon they are?'

'I can tell you that,' Jolie replied. 'A man called Kirby Taylor is behind them. He tried to kidnap me but I managed to get away. He owns all this land and the big house that goes with it.'

'There's no doubt that it's Kirby Taylor and his gang of gunslicks,' Shuman confirmed.

'Looks like we were right to have our suspicions,' Rattlesnake said.

'So what do we do now?' Shuman asked.

Wyeth's brows were puckered in concentration. 'Listen!' he said. They stopped talking and were quiet.

'No more shooting,' Rattlesnake said.

'That's right. I figure the varmints

have made a retreat. My guess is that they're makin' their way back to the house. There are probably more of 'em back there.' Wyeth turned to Jolie. 'How far is it to the house?'

'Hardly any distance.'

'I don't hear horses.'

'That's because they haven't got any,' Jolie replied. 'They came looking for me through the woods along the river.'

'Right,' Wyeth said. 'In that case, if we get the horses, we might be able to beat them to it.'

'What about Miss Rawley?' Shuman commented. 'Maybe we should leave Taylor be for now.'

'Don't worry about me,' Jolie said. 'I've got as much reason as the rest of you for dealing with Kirby Taylor. Probably more.'

'We can't give Taylor a chance to round up the rest of his men and get mounted. That would only put us in even more danger,' Wyeth said. 'We seem to have caught Taylor on the hop. Now's the time to deal with him before he gets organized.'

'We might be too late already,' Rattlesnake said.

'Then let's not waste any more time,' Jolie replied.

Wyeth looked at her. There was an air of determination about her that he had not seen before. 'Are you sure you're OK?' he said.

'I'm fine now I've found you,' she replied.

Wyeth looked at the others. 'Well,' he said, 'you heard the lady. Let's get mounted.'

It took only a few minutes for them to collect their horses. They climbed into leather, Jolie riding the steeldust with Wyeth, and covered the short distance to the covered bridge. The wooden walls and roof gave out a dull echo as they rode across. The bridge itself was shaded and they emerged at the opposite end into strong sunlight. The sun's rays glanced off something metallic and Wyeth realized that it was a rifle. The others had seen it, too. As the gun exploded Wyeth pushed Jolie down and dug in his spurs. Rattlesnake and Shuman had spread themselves low across their saddles. The first report was quickly followed by a further volley but the bullets flew high and wide. Once he was sure that he was out of range, Wyeth pulled hard on the reins.

'Stay with Rattlesnake and Shuman!' he yelled.

Without waiting for a reply, he vaulted out of the saddle. He had a good idea where the marksman was hidden in the trees alongside the river and he was suddenly maddened with rage. The man's bullet could have hit Jolie. He took no account of whether or not there might be more than one man concealed as he hurtled into the trees. He had gone temporarily berserk. He saw a flicker of movement in front of him as another shot rang out, tearing up the bark of a nearby tree. He ignored it, ploughing on and drawing his remaining six-gun. He saw something begin to move through the trees and understood from the accompanying sounds that whoever was concealed had taken to his heels. Yet another shot boomed but Wyeth ignored it. The trees were thick. He had lost sight of his quarry but he could hear the man crashing through the undergrowth.

He slowed for a moment before catching sight of him again. He was wearing a checked shirt. Wyeth had a flicker of memory. The man in the saloon who had quickly left on the night he had been bushwhacked had worn a distinctive checked shirt. Suddenly he was convinced that it was the same person. Maybe he had remained behind on the orders of Kirby Taylor, but more likely he had still been hoping to claim Wyeth as a victim for himself. Was he, after all, nothing but a bounty hunter? No, that couldn't be the case, or why would he be associated with Taylor? These thoughts flashed across Wyeth's mind as he bore down on his assailant.

The trees had thinned and he had a

clear view of the man. He was still carrying a rifle and, looking back towards Wyeth, he raised it to his shoulder and squeezed the trigger. The shot thudded into a tree but the move was his undoing. Not being careful to see what was in his path, he suddenly took a tumble. The rifle went flying from his grasp. He struggled to his feet but Wyeth flung himself on him and they both fell heavily to the ground. The man was up first. He swung a boot at Wyeth but Wyeth caught it and pushed him away. He staggered back and Wyeth was quickly on him, driving a fist into the man's solar plexus and following it up with a crashing blow to the jaw. The man reeled and his hand reached for his belt. In an instant he had pulled out a wicked-looking knife and as Wyeth came forward he slashed at him, catching him across the chest. Wyeth's jacket saved him from serious injury but he felt the sting of the blade. Ducking under the flailing knife, he brought his head up under the man's chin. His head snapped back and the knife slipped from his grip. Wyeth had him now. He landed another blow to the side of the man's face and he went down again. Wyeth dragged him back up and held him against a tree.

'OK,' he said, 'you'd better tell me what this is all about.' The man looked at him through bleary eyes.

'You hear what I say?' There was no response and Wyeth bashed his head against the tree. 'Start talkin',' he said. The man's eyes glazed over and Wyeth let him sink to the floor. He felt inside his jacket. There was something in his pocket and Wyeth knew what it was before he even withdrew it. It was a carved black skull. Wyeth held it in front of the hapless man before stretching out a hand to gather the knife.

'All right,' the man breathed. 'I'll talk. It was Taylor who put me up to it.'

'Kirby Taylor?'

'Yes. Taylor's the man behind it all.'

'Behind what?'

'The Black Skull.'

Wyeth shook him. 'You're not makin' yourself clear,' he said.

'Taylor formed the organization. He blamed the loss of the War on traitors. The Black Skull was formed to gain revenge on them. Anyone responsible for betraying the cause was to be killed.'

Wyeth was bewildered. 'What's that got to do with me?' he said. 'I fought on the side of the Confederacy. I rode with Jeb Stuart. I was in it from the start. Hell, I never even surrendered. I'm still carryin' it on.'

'I don't know. I just know he marked you down to die. He said you were one of the people who had betrayed the cause.'

'And you took on the job of carryin' out his instructions. Tell me, did you have somethin' to do with that varmint who tried to drygulch me back in Winding?'

The man nodded, wincing with pain as he did so. Wyeth got to his feet and began to walk away. He had only gone a few steps when he heard the sound of a gun being cocked behind him. He spun round. The man had a derringer in his hand. As he fired, Wyeth instinctively threw the knife he was still carrying. He felt the bullet sing by him and ducked away, but there was no second shot. When he looked back, the man lay on his back with the knife buried in his chest. Cautiously Wyeth approached, but there was nothing to be said or done. Zip Short was dead. Wyeth paused for a moment, standing over the body, before slipping the black skull he still held into his pocket.

After a few moments Wyeth turned and began to make his way back through the trees. His mind was in a whirl. He couldn't make sense of the man's references to the Black Skull. How could anyone accuse him of being a traitor? How could anyone think such a thing? The cause of the Confederacy was what he had fought for during those long years. It was what still inspired him, what still made him fight on. So how could it be that a supporter of the Confederacy would turn against another to the extent of wanting to kill him? It was the Union that was the enemy. He staggered on through the trees till he heard voices. They brought him back to reality and in a few moments he saw Rattlesnake and Shuman approaching, together with Jolie.

'What got into you?' Rattlesnake said.

Wyeth gave him a vague look. 'I got the varmint,' he said.

'Hell, you could have got yourself killed goin' off like that,' Rattlesnake retorted. 'As it is you're plumb lucky to be alive.'

'There was more than one of them,' Shuman said.

'There ain't any more,' Rattlesnake added. 'We dealt with 'em.' Wyeth realized he had been so intent on the chase that he hadn't heard any gunshots.

'Let's get to the horses,' he said.

It was only a short ride to the house.

When they got almost within sight of it, they drew to a halt and sat their horses.

'No sign of anybody,' Rattlesnake said.

'They must be in there, just waitin' for us. I guess that little incident down by the river slowed us up some.'

'I wonder how many of them there are?' Wyeth said.

'At least three less than when they started,' Rattlesnake commented.

Wyeth was thinking. Maybe Shuman was right. Maybe they should abandon the idea of dealing with Taylor, at least for the time being. He didn't like to leave unfinished business, but Taylor was in a strong position. He had made it back to his stronghold. What would he be expecting them to do? He had left three of his gunnies behind to deal with them, but would he be prepared for the eventuality that they would not succeed? Most likely, even if that was the case, he would expect them to make good their escape. It would make sense for them to ride away. But Wyeth had a score to settle with Taylor, and he was reluctant to turn away now. As he thought about the situation, an idea began to dawn in his mind.

'It sure is some mansion,' Rattlesnake mused.

'I reckon Taylor must have some real nice things in there,' Shuman commented.

'It should make a real nice fire.'

Wyeth turned to them. 'I appreciate what you boys are saying,' he responded, 'but I got something else in mind.' Jolie looked anxious. 'Have you ever heard of an organization called the Black Skull?' he asked.

The others shook their heads. 'No, neither had I till today,' Wyeth continued. 'Seems like it's some sort of assassination squad and Taylor's the ringleader.'

'Where did you find out about this?'

'The man who took that potshot turned out to be the same man who tried to back-shoot me in Cold Creek. He was probably responsible for the dynamiting, too. I got it from him.'

'I don't understand,' Rattlesnake said.

'No, neither do I. Not properly. But I aim to find out more from the man himself.'

'What? You mean Taylor?'

'Yes, that's exactly who I mean. It shouldn't be too hard to get into that house. It'll be the last thing Taylor would expect any of us to do.'

'You're goin' to try it alone? It's too dangerous,' Rattlesnake remarked.

'No more dangerous than any of the other things we've been doin' for years now.'

'I agree with Rattlesnake,' Jolie said. 'Please don't try and enter that house by yourself.'

Wyeth looked into her troubled eyes. 'Don't worry,' he said, 'It'll be a piece of cake. I won't be taking any unnecessary chances. I got too much to live for now.'

She made as if she would argue with him but something about Wyeth's demeanour made her see the pointlessness of attempting to dissuade him.

'Try the library,' she said. 'It's where he tried to shut me up.' She gave the best description she could of the house and its layout.

'Please, please be careful,' she concluded.

'Thanks,' Wyeth said. 'That's real helpful.'

'What about Taylor?' Shuman said. 'You don't know what he looks like.'

'There's no mistaking him,' Jolie said and gave a shudder.

'You're right,' Shuman replied, but proceeded to give a description of Taylor anyway. Wyeth listened closely before dismounting.

'Keep out of sight,' he told the others.

'How long do we give you?' Rattlesnake said.

Wyeth shrugged. 'Just be ready to back me up if I need you,' he replied.

He slipped away. All his knowledge and experience of guerrilla warfare came to his aid as he moved swiftly and stealthily towards the big house. To his practised eye the seemingly open spaces in front offered plenty of cover. When he reached the house he flattened himself against the wall and, taking account of what Jolie had told him, inched his way around the side till he came to some windows. If he and Jolie had worked things out right, this should be the library. He ducked low and then raised his head above the window ledge. Jolie had guessed correctly. He was in luck. Inside the room a man was sitting at a desk. Jolie had been right about his appearance too. There was no doubt in his mind that the man was Kirby Taylor.

He was not alone. Standing by the door was one of his gunslicks. Wyeth dropped down and thought for a moment before drawing his six-gun and rapping it against the window. He would have liked to see the reaction but he had a pretty good idea of what it would be. He waited, tensed for action.

After a few moments there was a noise at the window sash and the window began to rise. A head appeared, leaning out. In a flash Wyeth was on his feet as he brought the barrel of his pistol crashing down on the gunnie's skull. He gave a low moan and then fell backwards. Instantly Wyeth put his foot on the windowsill and leaped into the room. The action had been so quick that Taylor had barely time to rise to his feet before being presented with the muzzle of Wyeth's .44.

'Don't make a sound,' Wyeth hissed.

Taylor's eyes flickered for a moment towards the door. Focusing his attention on Taylor, Wyeth backed towards it. The key was in the lock and he turned it.

'Well,' he said, 'it looks like it's just you and me.' Taylor's face had turned white. He tried to say something but the words wouldn't come.

'Guess you know who I am,' Wyeth said. Taylor did not reply. 'I know something about you as well,' Wyeth continued, 'but you got a lot of explaining to do.' He glanced at the drinks cabinet. 'Might as well make ourselves comfortable,' he said. 'Why don't you go over there and pour a couple of drinks? Whiskey will be fine. And remember, I got this gun pointed right at you. I wouldn't advise you to make any sudden moves.'

He wasn't expecting Taylor to do anything of the kind. The man seemed to be struck immobile and it was only when Wyeth encouraged him with a wave of the gun that he jerked into a semblance of animation, walking like an automaton to the cabinet. With trembling fingers he poured whiskey into one glass, spilling some as he did so.

'I must insist that you join me,' Wyeth said. 'I hate to drink alone.'

Taylor reached for another glass and poured a second drink. When he had finished he looked bemusedly at Wyeth.

'Take them over to the desk,' Wyeth said. With one hand he pulled out a chair and when Taylor had placed the drinks on the table, he pushed him into it. Wyeth himself took the chair that Taylor had been occupying. It gave him a good view of the room and the door and also allowed him to look outside. The gunslick he had buffaloed lay inert nearby. When they were seated he took a sip of whiskey and looked hard at Taylor's blanched features.

'Tell me about the Black Skull,' he said.

'Black Skull,' Taylor mumbled. 'I don't know what you're talking about.'

'I think you do,' Wyeth replied. He reached into his pocket and produced the little carving he had taken from Short. He held it on the palm of his hand for a moment before passing it to Taylor.

'I don't understand,' he stammered. 'What is this? Where did you get it?'

'That don't matter,' Wyeth said. He drew back the hammer of his .44. 'I'm countin' to ten. If you don't start comin' clean, I'm going to shoot you.'

'You wouldn't do that,' Taylor said in

a sudden half-hearted moment of defiance. 'Once they hear a noise, my boys will come running.'

'I think we've accounted for quite a few of your gun-totin' owlhoots,' Wyeth replied. He began counting. 'One, two, three, four . . . ' He extended his arm and pointed the gun so it was close to Taylor's forehead.

'All right, all right,' Taylor gasped. 'I'll talk. I have heard of the Black Skull, but I swear it's nothing to do with me.'

Wyeth lowered his arm. 'All I know,' Taylor continued, 'is that the Black Skull is some kind of secret organization.'

'Go on.'

'That's it. It's only what I heard.'

Wyeth looked around the room. He allowed his eyes to rest for a moment on the solitary bookcase and the picture hanging over it. There was a movement from Taylor and when Wyeth glanced at him he could see a bead of sweat running down his brow.

'Somethin' troublin' you?' he asked.

Taylor didn't respond and Wyeth turned his attention back to the large painting.

'That's an interestin' picture,' he said. 'What is it?'

Taylor swallowed. 'It's a scene from Norse mythology. It depicts the arrival in Valhalla of a fallen hero accompanied by valkyries.'

Wyeth got to his feet and walked towards it. Taylor swallowed hard once again. He was clearly uncomfortable and as he got close to the painting Wyeth began to understand why.

'Well now,' he said as he stood beside it. 'It sure is a nice painting, but there seems to be somethin' else here.' He reached up and moved the painting slightly. There was something behind; the painting had obviously been artfully hung in that spot in order to conceal it. It was a safe. Wyeth's face was grim as he turned back to Taylor.

'Open it!' he snapped.

Taylor's face seemed to have melted.

Drops of sweat ran down it and it had the consistency of putty.

'There's nothing in it,' he mumbled. 'It was there before I took over the place.'

Wyeth raised his gun. 'Open it. Now.'

Taylor fumbled in a drawer and produced a key. Getting to his feet, he crossed the room and inserted it in the lock.

'Take out any papers,' Wyeth said.

'There's nothing of any interest.'

'Do as I say.'

For a moment Taylor continued to hold back before reaching into the safe and pulling out a number of documents.

'Take 'em over to the table,' Wyeth ordered.

Taylor gathered them up. When he had placed them on the table and taken his seat again, Wyeth riffled through them with the barrel of his gun. He pushed one forward in front of Taylor.

'Start reading,' he said.

Taylor ran his hand through his hair.

'All right,' he said. 'I don't need to read anything. All the proof you want is in those documents. What do you want from me? You're right. I formed the Black Skull.'

'For what purpose?'

'You fought for the Confederacy,' Taylor began to wheedle. 'You know how it was. You know that the Union could never have beaten us if we had stood firm.'

'For what purpose?'

'Traitors deserve to die,' Taylor almost screamed. He was growing increasingly agitated. 'I am a patriot. I deserve better than this.'

'You had me down as a traitor,' Wyeth said. 'You marked me out for execution.' His face was a mask of contempt. 'I don't understand your twisted reasons. Try and explain it to me. How could you think I was a traitor?'

'You were with Jeb Stuart. It was because of you that we lost at Gettysburg. That was the turning point.

If you had shown up in time, we could have won.'

'You're crazy,' Wyeth said.

'You were too late for Gettysburg. Too late for Gettysburg!' Taylor was beginning to foam at the mouth. He seemed to have forgotten his situation as he struggled to his feet.

'You deserve to die. You and everyone else who failed that day. Too late for Gettysburg, but not too late to be punished; not too late to die.'

Wyeth was fascinated, trying to understand the man's reasoning. He was so intent that he did not register the fact that the gunnie lying on the floor had come round. Only when he let out an involuntary groan as he reached for his gun did Wyeth react. As the man's pistol exploded he threw himself aside. The bullet smashed into his arm, causing him to drop the .44.

'Quick!' Taylor shouted frantically. 'Shoot him! Shoot him again!'

The words served to galvanize Wyeth. Before the gunnie could fire again, he kicked the gun out of his hand. Wyeth made a dive to reach it. At almost the same moment a shot rang out. Taylor had picked up Wyeth's gun. Wyeth rolled sideways and as a second bullet thudded into the floor he took a moment to steady himself before squeezing the trigger of the gunslick's pistol. The shot sent Taylor spinning back. Outside the door Wyeth could hear the clatter of boots.

'Are you OK?' someone shouted.

Taylor was leaning against the wall. He raised Wyeth's gun and fired again, but Wyeth was too quick. As Taylor's bullet shattered the window, Wyeth's found its mark. His skull shattered, Taylor slid slowly to the floor while his expression of shock and bewilderment seemed to linger behind. Fists were thumping on the door and as he got to his feet, Wyeth felt the gunnie's hand close around his ankle. He kicked it aside and made a dive for the window. He flew through it head first, cutting his leg as he did so on a shard of glass.

He hit the ground hard but was quickly up and running. Another gunslick appeared to bar his way and Wyeth fired. The man fell back and Wyeth hurtled on. Shots began to ring out both behind and in front of him and he assumed that he was surrounded. Then he realized that the shots in front were coming from Rattlesnake and Shuman. They were running towards him with guns blazing. In a moment the shots from behind became more sporadic. Wyeth glanced back. There were only two or three gunnies left on their feet and they were running pell-mell towards the back of the house.

'We got 'em!' Rattlesnake yelled.

Wyeth stopped in his tracks as the others came alongside. Shuman ran past, carrying on shooting, but there was no one left to fire at. As they stood they heard the sound of horses snorting and then the rattle of hoofs.

'I guess they've had enough,' Rattlesnake said.

Wyeth was panting, trying to gather

his breath. 'They probably realize that Taylor's dead,' he muttered.

'What happened?' Rattlesnake said. He looked more closely at Wyeth.

'Hell, you're bleeding,' he said. 'You've been hit.'

Wyeth looked down at his arm. In the heat of battle, he had been unaware of his injury. 'It's nothin' much,' he said. 'I'll be OK.'

Before Rattlesnake could reply, Wyeth looked up again and his heart thumped. Walking towards him was Jolie Rawley. Rattlesnake observed the look on his face.

'Oh yes,' he said. 'Jolie was right there alongside us but I guess we pressed ahead a little too fast.'

Wyeth began to run and so did Jolie. In a few moments he had reached her and taken her into his arms. Rattlesnake and Shuman stood together watching them.

'Guess he can't be too badly injured,' Shuman said. 'Not the way he's got hold of her.'

'Nope, but then I reckon he wouldn't feel it right now if a cannonball had hit him. Hell, maybe it has.' The two men chuckled. 'You know,' Rattlesnake resumed, 'I didn't get a chance to go into details, but I guess we won't be havin' any more trouble from Taylor.'

★   ★   ★

Night had descended on the town of Winding. A thin shaving of moon hung above the garden of the Holland house where a crowd of people sat at table. The whole family were gathered, together with their guests, Rattlesnake Jack and Shuman. Wyeth, his arm bandaged, sat close to Jolie.

'Ma,' he said, 'that was the best meat pie I've tasted for years.'

'Well, that wouldn't be too surprising,' she replied. 'Now don't anyone stand on ceremony. Help yourself to seconds.'

'Ma'am, you read my thoughts,' Rattlesnake replied.

When they had all had their fill and the plates were cleared, they settled down to enjoy a big pot of coffee.

'It's good to have you back, Sam,' Shelby said. 'You sure had us worried when you disappeared last time.'

'I'm sorry about that,' Wyeth replied. 'It won't happen again.'

His mother turned on him. 'How can we be sure of that?' she said.

'Isn't it obvious?' Kate laughed.

Wyeth and Jolie exchanged glances. 'Of course Jolie's the main reason,' Wyeth said, 'but it's not just that. I've been doin' a lot of thinkin' recently.'

Shelby leaned forward. 'I figured somethin' had happened,' he said. 'You seem different somehow.'

'I've told you something about what happened back there in Cold Creek. What I couldn't understand was how anyone would be so twisted as to blame people like me and Rattlesnake for losing the war. I'm not sure how to put it, but if that was the case, then what was I still fighting for? I don't know; it just hit me hard.'

'I'd say it made you see sense,' his mother replied.

Kate made a motion to quieten her, but Wyeth took up her words. 'Ma's right,' he said. 'I've been a fool. I've been a fool and worse ever since the war ended. Well, it's time I put that right. You might say I've finally surrendered.'

'I'm glad you feel that way,' Kate said. She hesitated, reluctant to bring up the question that was on everyone's mind. It was Wyeth himself who brought it out into the open.

'I know what you're thinkin'. I'm a wanted man. I got a price on my head. Well, I guess I got to do the right thing. I'm going to hand myself in.'

'No,' Rattlesnake exclaimed. 'You can't do that. They'll put you away. We can do like we said and head for the Nations or maybe Texas. You'd be safe there. Nobody would ask any questions.'

'It wouldn't be right. It wouldn't even be fair on you. I'm the one with a price on his head.'

'Don't say that,' Rattlesnake said. 'We've rode together for too long to be thinkin' that way.'

There was a heavy pause before Wyeth's mother spoke. 'I've already had a word with Marshal Snider,' she said. 'Don't get me wrong. I haven't said anything about Sam being here. As far as he's concerned, Sam could already be in Texas or anywhere else. We spoke in general terms. But he's a good man. He's known Sam since he was a kid. He has some sympathy for his cause. Remember, Sam hasn't killed anyone and all the money he's taken has been used in good causes, like the money from that last bank job.'

'Thanks for my share of that,' Shuman interpolated. 'It'll sure help set me up again in Winding. Maybe I'll even make a proper doctor.'

'Like I say, the marshal's sympathetic. He'll do what he can to get Sam a pardon and I, for one, reckon he'll do it.'

'Thanks, Ma,' Wyeth said.

'I still don't like it,' Rattlesnake said. His face suddenly brightened. 'Hell,' he added, 'if things don't work out, I reckon I could bust you free!'

His words brought a sense of relief to the group. Wyeth turned to Jolie.

'You'll wait for me?' he said.

She looked at him through bright eyes. 'Of course I will,' she said. 'After all, I've waited for you all this time. But I don't reckon it will be for much longer.'

Shelby looked towards his brother. 'I figure you're doing the right thing,' he said.

'Yeah,' Wyeth replied. 'It's strange, but I'm feeling a whole lot better already. It's like Eugene Wyeth just died and Sam Holland's been born again.'

THE END